VALUE FOR MURDER

VALUE FOR MURDER

Overhead, the army chopper dropped closer to the cabin. Outside in the darkness the police waited for the kidnappers to emerge. The car was parked a few yards from the cabin, and if Brad could only reach it he might rate a chance of escape. He knew there would be a certain amount of risk involved – you didn't pick up a quarter of a million dollars by playing it safe. Brad hadn't minded the risk, so long as he lived through it to enjoy the money, but the scheme had gone horribly wrong...

VALUE FOR MURDER

by

Craig Cooper

Dales Large Print Books
Long Preston, North Yorkshire,
BD23 4ND, England.

British Library Cataloguing in Publication Data.

Cooper, Craig
    Value for murder.

    A catalogue record of this book is
    available from the British Library

    ISBN   1-84262-475-X pbk
    ISBN   978-1-84262-475-3 pbk

First published in Great Britain in 1972 by
Robert Hale & Company

Copyright © Craig Cooper 1972

The moral right of the author has been asserted

Published in Large Print 2006 by arrangement with
Robert Hale Limited

Dales Large Print is an imprint of Library Magna Books Ltd.

Printed and bound in Great Britain by
T.J. (International) Ltd., Cornwall, PL28 8RW

CHAPTER ONE

They found Bradford Gilbert playing pool in a hall on Denver Avenue, or rather, Roy Judge found him there. Brad Gilbert was a trim six-footer, wide in the shoulders, and with a tough, aggressive nature. A product of the wrong side of the tracks, he had done just about every menial job there was in his time. Then came induction and Vietnam, and Brad Gilbert discovered something else about himself in relation to the world in general. His uniform gave him a sense of pride and belonging. It was as though he had been plucked from oblivion and endowed with a significance he had never dreamed possible.

In the army he walked straight and tall, prideful and self-contained, and while it couldn't be said he enjoyed the jungle warfare, he had derived a vast satisfaction from knowing he was wanted and needed and that in some odd fashion he was participating in the moulding of history.

Brad caught a bullet in the right leg in an ambush and that was that. He spent two months in hospital suffering operations involving bone grafts, and then he was out of the army and back home in his bachelor diggings in Kentburg.

For a while he walked with a limp and earned the name Limpy. That sobriquet died a swift death on the night he broke the jaw of a boozed-up freeloader in Mason's bar on Fourth Avenue.

He returned to the job he had had prior to his call-up – driving a truck for Trans-West Transport. One night he was hijacked with a consignment of cigarettes and tobacco. The cops found him on the roadside after the truck was reported missing, with a lump the size of an egg on his skull. Brad spent a week on free pay, but a little later it was noticed he was flashing more money around than his earnings as a truck driver warranted. The upshot was he was fired on a flimsy pretext. It took a few months for the cops to get off his back and stop following him everywhere he went.

Roy Judge, who walked into the frowzy atmosphere of the pool hall that night, was a man in his late twenties. He was thin and wiry-looking, with gaunt features and dark eyes. He was bony, without much muscle apparent on his lean frame, and yet he gave the impression of a coiled whiplash, ready to become taut and flash out in explosive temper with little provocation. He was dressed jazzily, in a yellow no-iron shirt, tan sport jacket and cream trousers. He stuck up like a pansy in a bed of weeds from the other habitués of the pool hall.

Judge watched the play at the tables for a while. He didn't go for pool and the sight bored him. Then, when Brad was standing back, lighting a cigarette and chalking his cue, he moved in at the big man's elbow.

'Hi there, Brad. I'd like a word with you.'

Brad glanced at him and frowned.

'Oh, hello, Roy.'

He put the chalk away and licked the tips of his fingers. He blinked from the smoke curling up around his eyes.

'You busy?' Judge said with meagre humour.

What is it?'

'We can't natter here, Brad. Come on over to Gilly's bar.'

'I don't think I feel like it, Roy. I'm making out okay. Buzz off like a good guy.'

Judge's small mouth tightened and he balled his hands in his pockets.

'Look, Brad, I'm not kidding. This is important. Jack Royal sent me. You know Jack, Brad. When he sends a message to a man he expects that message to be delivered.'

'Oh, knot Royal,' Brad said angrily. 'He hasn't got me on a string.'

Judge's eyes glittered like black beads. He coughed in the putrid atmosphere.

'Suit yourself, friend. But I wouldn't be in your shoes for a million bucks.'

He was cutting out for the door when

Brad spoke after him. 'Wait, Roy.'

'Come on, Brad,' his opponent complained. 'You want all night to study it?'

Brad's eyes flickered to Sol Birch. He smiled faintly. 'Sorry, I've got to go.' He put his cue in the rack, lifted his jacket, and went to the door after Roy Judge.

Judge went on through and crossed the crowded, neon-lit street in front of him, heading for Gilly's bar.

They took a booth at the back of the bar and Judge ordered bourbon for both of them. Waiting for the drinks to arrive he considered the man before him.

Judge had a sneaking admiration for Brad as a physical specimen that he wouldn't admit in a hundred years. He thought Brad was the type who could have made a good movie star. He had poise and self-assurance and was equipped with the kind of rugged handsomeness that most women went for. But underlying the grudging admiration was a generous contempt. The man should have made something out of himself before now. He didn't have the brains, Judge guessed. He was destined to drive a truck or wield a pick-axe and never to get to the top of anything.

Intelligence was the key, Judge told himself. You either had it or you hadn't, and if you hadn't got intelligence you deserved to spend your life being the tool of other, cleverer people. Like Jack Royal, Judge

10

reflected. He wanted to do a job and he required a man of the calibre of Brad, a man who had been tested for courage and nerve and who had come through the test, so he put out an order to get Brad.

Brad Gilbert didn't think much about the man opposite him at all. Roy Judge was a volatile showoff who bragged about the women he had taken and the places he was going to. One of these days Roy was going to go into a prison cell so fast he would bust his nose on the wall facing the door. Brad could take Roy or leave him. He got along with most anybody so long as they didn't dig too deep under his skin.

The drinks arrived and Judge proposed a toast.

'To great things, Brad,' he said with his sly grin. 'Hows about that, old timer. Great things. Too bad those bastards kicked you out of the trucking company. But who wants to drive a truck anyway?'

'You couldn't blame them,' Brad said equably. 'If you were running a business you wouldn't keep a man who was gypping you.'

'Yes. But that's their angle. You don't waste sympathy on the other guy, for pete's sake.'

'All the same, you're smart if you can look at his side of the affair. Did you ask me here to talk about the hijack effort?'

'No, you're wrong, Brad.'

'I got my cut and I never complained.'

11

'But you haven't got a job at the moment, Brad. I mean, a few thousand bucks won't keep you for ever. A man needs capital. You get no place in this world without capital.'

Brad thought he was a naïve jerk.

'So?' he murmured over the rim of his glass. 'If you join the capitalists you become an enemy of the commies and the socialists.'

'You fought the commies, Brad.'

'I fought a lot of guys without faces, without bodies. Spooks that came and went in the greenery. I didn't want to fight them. If I became a capitalist all these commies might start ganging up on me.'

Judge stared at him, his lips peeled away from his teeth in a disbelieving snarl. He wondered if Bradford Gilbert had lost some of his marbles since the hijack stunt.

'You're joking me, Brad,' he said with a neighing laugh. 'You're talking a load of crap.'

'Let's get back to the point, Roy. Tell Jack I'm making out okay. It was nice of him to cut me in before. But I'm not sticking my neck out again for a pocketful of any man's peanuts.'

'Peanuts!' Judge scoffed. 'Oh, no, Brad friend, you're wrong. This is it, brother. If we pull it off we're on easy street from here to eternity.'

'I'm not interested, Roy. You tell him that. Just say I'm not interested.'

Judge finished his drink and prepared to

rise. 'Okay, bum,' he said scornfully. 'If you haven't got the guts...'

Brad caught his elbow in a savage grip and slammed him back down on his seat. His grey eyes flared momentarily and his jaws bunched.

'Don't you call me that, big time. Mind your tongue or I'll smash your mouth.'

'Okay, Brad, okay. Don't bust any seams. Okay buddy. Comrade. You said it and I understood you. But like I told you, Jack is a hard man to cross. As hard as you, Brad.'

Judge was rising again when Brad said quickly, 'What is he planning to do?'

'It's his business, buddy. Comrade. If you're not in you're out. Is that all right with you?'

Brad's gaze went smoky with thought for a moment.

'No, wait,' he said less stiffly. 'I might think it over.'

'Why? Because you're scared of Jack?'

'Because I don't have much left of the dough. I was thinking of pulling out for the east,' he went on reflectively.

'That's a better tune, Brad. But it doesn't fill the bill. Jack says you do or you don't. But he does want you. Understand?'

'You make it sound like blossom time in the country, Roy.'

'It's nothing to trifle with. If you haven't got the heart for action there's no sense in straining yourself.'

'What's it all about?'

'Making a million dollars. Wish I could tell you more about it, Brad, but I can't. If you want to hear the rest be at Swift's Beach in–' Judge looked at the watch on his wrist and expressed surprise. 'Nearly ten. I didn't know it was so late. Jack wanted you there by ten-thirty.'

'Where? At that house where he coops up with his sister?'

Judge gave a shrill laugh.

'Darla kept talking about you after your last visit. Thought you were the bees' knees. That Darla dame certainly goes for you in a big way.'

Brad remembered the big, busty woman all right. She was about forty and her husband had died two or three years ago. The house she and Jack Royal occupied at Swift's Beach had been her husband's first of all; then he married Darla and took her home to it. Sime Grant had been a salesman and travelled all over the country. One day his car was in head-on collision with a creamery truck and he had been dead when they extricated him from the wreckage.

Afterwards Jack Royal, who had been a seaman for a few years, but who thought there was more money to be made by capitalising his wits and nerve, moved in with his sister. Darla Grant didn't mind sharing the house with her brother so long as he paid his way and could guarantee that she wouldn't have to go to prison with him when the cops eventually tumbled to his rackets.

'Yeah,' Judge went. 'Darla's house. Will you be there? Your car is okay?'

Brad nodded, thinking it over. He was at a loose end and his share of the hijack rake-off was steadily running out. When it did run out Myrna would forsake him and he would be on his own again. Unless he married Myrna. But he had no intention of marrying her. He was frightened of marriage and all that such a union with a woman entailed. She could take off if she wished, at any time she wished.

Judge was rising from the table.

'Just a minute, Roy. Supposing I didn't care for what Jack is setting up? What would I do then?'

Judge's black eyes oscillated over his face in a way that made Brad feel uneasy. He shrugged. He leaned down across the table and pitched his voice on a quiet note.

'If you listened to the dope and then refused to handle it you would have to take a long trip, Brad. Nothing more or less. As a precaution against being picked up by the cops, you understand. You do understand?'

Brad nodded. He looked glum. He had a way of looking glum when he was thinking deeply.

'Who else is there besides Jack, you and me?'

15

'Just Pete Kripp. You know Pete. He's a good guy. That's all. Only the four of us.'

'All right,' Brad said. 'There's no reason why I can't give it a whirl. I'll be at the Beach shortly.'

Judge grinned, slapped his shoulder and left him.

Brad smoked for a few minutes after Judge had gone. He thought of his position and measured it against whatever deal Jack Royal had in mind. What did Royal have in mind, he wondered. There was only one way to find out.

He left the bar presently, walking along the street to get his beat-up Dodge. In the car he drove the ten miles to the coast and Swift's Beach.

It was raining by the time he arrived at the Beach. The fun houses fronting the beach itself were going full blast. The roar of the breakers beating on the nearby cliffs was thunderous in his ears as he parked the Dodge at the elevated frame building. There were two other cars squatting in the shadow of the house, fresher models than his own, slick and gleaming in the wet.

Brad went up the creaking steps to the back porch and rapped on the screen door. It was opened by Darla who smiled widely at him. She was wearing a halter and tight Capri pants so that the bulges of her bosom and hips were accentuated to the full. She was fair, like her brother, with good strong features and generous, sensual mouth. Brad got a whiff of scent that was comprised of perfume and gin.

He said politely, 'Is your brother at home, Mrs. Grant?'

'Yes, he's here, of course, Bradford. You don't mind if I call you Bradford?'

Her bosom was practically glued to his chest as she spoke and Brad grinned faintly, aware of a stir in his veins.

'Not at all. But I'd rather you called me Brad.'

They laughed and she hesitated for a moment, reluctant to give him up to the others just yet.

'Then you'll call me Darla?'

The scene was becoming slightly ridiculous. Both of them were long past kid-stuff of this nature.

'If you say so. Look,' he added more briskly, 'I think Jack is waiting for me...'

Her manner changed. She adopted a worried expression. She laid a hand on Brad's arm.

'They're cooking up something, Brad. Do you know what it is?'

'Uh-uh! Haven't got a clue. But I wouldn't get steamed up about anything if I were you. We–'

A door down the hall opened and Jack Royal thrust his head out to squint at them standing in the shadows.

'Darla, is that Brad? Why the hell are you keeping him standing there?'

'Oh, dry up, Jack, and when you do blow away. You take me for your little black slave, you'd better get a bunch of better ideas.'

'Come on in, Brad. What about fixing some coffee, slave girl? Make it for three. Pete doesn't want any. Look, Brad, I said to come on in, didn't I?'

Brad went along the hall to meet Jack Royal.

Royal was a heavily-built man, short and compact, and with his barrel chest and thick neck he gave the impression of tremendous strength. His hair was flecked with grey; it was thinning and disappearing at the temples. He had a high, wide forehead, small, closely-spaced eyes that were a pale blue shade and reminded Brad of cold steel. The nose was strong and large and flared slightly at the nostrils. His mouth was a meagre, unimaginative slash. Right now Royal was dressed in a lightweight brown suit that was rumpled and in need of cleaning. The jacket strained under his arms and across his chest. A white handkerchief was stuffed carelessly in the breast pocket.

Roy Judge and Pete Knipp were taking it easy in lounging chairs. Judge grinned and gave Brad a welcoming thumbs-up sign.

Kripp said, 'Hello, Brad,' and raised a hand

negligently as if he was sapped of energy.

Kripp was around Brad's age, which was thirty. He was sallow-featured, with large tar-dark eyes and too-thick lips. He was wearing a cream sport suit and his straw hat lay at the floor by his feet. He had large white teeth which he flashed briefly before drawing the rubbery lips over them. Brad had an odd, indefinable aversion to Kripp.

They sat there and smoked until Darla came in with the coffee. Having served Brad and moving away from him she flirted her round hips at him and when the door closed on her Brad found himself looking into Jack Royal's eyes.

'That dame has a big yen for you, Brad.'

'What am I supposed to do – blush? Roy said you had business to discuss.'

'That's right, pal, I have. But before we move another step, I want to get one point crystal clear. If I tell you what I'm planning and you decide you haven't got the stomach for it, then an embarrassing situation is going to arise.'

'Roy explained that,' Brad said curtly. 'I thought it over before I came here.'

'So now that you are here it means you have committed yourself?'

'More or less. Of course I won't have anything to do with a murder rap, Jack. Even my guts aren't that strong. There's still a lot of living I've got to do.'

Judge emitted a faint snigger. Pete Kripp brought a thin cigar from a pocket of his vest and lit it. The ghost of a smile flitted over Jack Royal's full face.

He shook his head.

'Nuts to that, Brad. I may be a pile of things but I'm not a complete weirdo. What would your reaction be if I said we have set up a glorious snatch?'

Brad was thoughtfully silent for a few minutes. At last he said, 'What do you call glorious, Jack? Roy was talking in terms of a million dollars.'

'Roy wasn't kidding,' Jack said bluntly. 'This is where you walk out of here and vanish or sit where you are and pin your ears back.'

'If it's a juvenile, I'm out. I wouldn't touch it under any circumstances.'

'It isn't a juvenile. It's an adult. Make up your mind quickly now. Yes or no?'

Brad was aware of the tension building about him. Kripp was puffing smoke rings from his cigar. Judge was working at his nails with a file. But the pressure of their thoughts was almost tangible.

'A four-way split?' Brad murmured at length.

'What else?' Royal growled roughly. 'Okay, let's get down to the bare bones and sort them out.'

CHAPTER TWO

It was a fantastic idea that Royal had conceived, and the sheer enormity of it caused Brad to catch his breath as the squat man unfolded his scheme.

Kripp and Judge had apparently been through the whole thing already, and they merely sat back and listened idly while Jack Royal talked.

The plan consisted of snatching Carol Regan, the daughter of the oil millionaire, Wesley Regan, and holding her to ransom to the tune of a million dollars. In essence, this was what they intended doing, and when Royal had dropped his bombshell on Brad he waited for his comments.

'Kidnap Carol Regan!' Brad marvelled and gave vent to an incredulous laugh that put a tide of dark colour to crawling through Royal's cheeks.

'What's so hilarious?' he demanded. He plucked a cigarette from a silver case and trapped it in his tight mouth, giving Brad time to pull himself together.

'What the hell isn't funny?' Brad retorted. 'You'd never make it in the first place. Even if you did manage to snatch the dame, what would you do with her? Where would you take her? Here for Darla to look after until the dough is handed over? I can see Darla doing it, too. I don't think.'

'Don't be stupid.'

Brad turned his head to see Pete Kripp studying him from behind the cigar smoke. Brad stared at him and was angered by the contempt in those tar-black eyes.

'I figured this was Jack I was talking with,' he said ominously. 'Can Jack not speak for himself?'

'You want to drive one of your trucks through it, don't you?'

Kripp went on needling him.

'For crying out loud!' Judge griped in disgust. 'You two guys start pulling each other's hair and we might as well call it off. Ease up, Pete.'

'Okay, so it isn't funny,' Brad said, breathing heavily. 'It isn't funny by a mile. And that's what I mean when I say you'll never make it.'

'Shut up,' Royal rapped at him. 'Are you scared, Brad?'

'I'm not a bumhead, Jack.'

'But are you scared?' Royal persisted.

'No, I'm not scared.'

'I didn't think you would be,' the squat man grunted. 'So just listen. We will make it. We're going to make it. I've set up more deals than you know about, Brad,' he went on with great earnestness. 'I'm not a punk who'll risk my skin on the toss of a coin. Do you know that?'

'I'll take your word for it,' Brad said. He attempted a smile that didn't really come off.

'Get one thing clear at the outset,' Royal told him. 'Darla. She's okay and we get along, but she's only a woman. Understand? She hasn't heard about this. She isn't going to hear about it. Now or at any time later. We four are the only people who are in on the trick. It's got to be sewed up tight at that point.'

Brad sobered then, realising for the first time what he had actually let himself in for. But supposing they did happen to pull it off, his thoughts raced on. A million bucks. Split four ways. Two hundred and fifty thousand dollars apiece. It was staggering. With that sort of money he could move on to easy street for the rest of his natural.

Regarding Jack Royal's ability to plan a deal and carry it through to a successful conclusion – well, he had made a success of the hijack thing, had he not? All would have gone well had he not flashed his money too soon. If there had been a crack in that scheme he was solely responsible for it. But it hadn't gone so far for the cops to pull him in and accuse him of anything. All they could do was suspect him of being implicated. And certainly suspicion had never centred on Jack Royal or these other two guys.

'You've got a plan worked out thoroughly?' he asked in a more subdued voice.

Jack Royal nodded. His annoyance melted slowly from his features. He was ready to make allowances for Brad's dogged scepticism.

'Do you know what Carol Regan looks like?' he asked Brad.

Brad had to think about this.

'Yeah, I believe I do. I saw a photo in the paper a few weeks ago. Old Wesley was throwing a big party at his home on Seaway Heights. There was a whole page of photos. She's a blonde girl, isn't she?'

Instead of answering, Jack Royal took a large manila envelope from a drawer and withdrew a sheaf of newspaper cuttings. They were all photographs and in each of them Wesley Regan's daughter was featured.

He dropped them before Brad and told him to look at them closely. Brad did so. Carol Regan was a rare dish, he thought. Tall, statuesque and blonde. Stacked like all his dream girls were stacked.

'Man oh man!' he said presently. 'If this beauty isn't worth a million bucks I don't know what is.'

Royal glanced at the other two in the lounging chairs. They were watching Brad but they acknowledged the squat man's gaze.

'You couldn't possibly mistake her now?'

'Who, me?' Brad raised his head from the clippings and grinned at Royal. 'You bet I wouldn't. But here, what has it got to do with me especially?'

'I'll tell you,' Royal said.

He gathered up the clippings in a bundle in his huge fist and took them to the fireplace. There was no fire but Royal made one of the clippings with his lighter. He came back to his chair and sat down. His pale blue eyes held Brad's.

'This is Tuesday night,' he began. 'Tonight the dame's boy-friend calls at the house and takes her out on a date. He does the same thing tomorrow night. On Thursday night the dame is driven to The Art Academy on Second Avenue.'

'That's some kind of school for amateur actors, isn't it?'

'It's a high-tone joint where aspiring actors with more money than acting ability go to be taught stage training,' Royal explained. 'Like I said, she is driven there by one of Regan's uniformed flunkies. He drops her at the Academy at seven-thirty sharp and calls back for her two and a half hours later at ten.'

'She doesn't drive a car herself?'

'She used to drive but she had an accident.

She crashed a car and was unconscious in hospital for two days. She must have made a good recovery, but whatever way her old man took it, he didn't let her drive again.'

'So Wesley Regan is some kind of kook?'

'I don't know what kind of kook he is. But this illustrates how he feels about his daughter. He lost his wife in a driving accident and he's going to make sure he doesn't lose his daughter in one.'

Brad thought it all over for a little. He didn't see the logic in it. Carol Regan could be involved in a car accident with her boyfriend at the wheel or with a chauffeur just as easily as if she were driving herself.

'You seem to have been doing your homework, Jack.'

'Yeah, I have.' Royal's grin was wry. 'For the past couple of months. Now, Brad, on Thursday night at nine o'clock you're going to drive up to the front of the Academy in the same kind of Cadillac that transports the dame to and from it. You'll go into the hall and inform the doorman that Miss Regan is required at home immediately as her father is ill.'

That was where he came in, Brad thought with a jolt.

'Why me, Jack?'

'It ought to be obvious,' Roy Judge interposed with his neighing laugh. 'Can you imagine me in polished boots and silver buttons? Or Pete? Or Jack?'

Brad couldn't. All the same he didn't have to ask who was taking the biggest risk, who would be left holding the baby if the plot should slip out of gear. And what if the slip occurred before he managed to get the girl clear?

'Where do I take her?' he said tautly. 'Assuming that the gag works and she gets into the car, and she doesn't decide to bring a friend along for the ride.'

'She won't have any friend along. I told you, she goes there alone and she leaves alone.'

'But she's going to catch on pretty soon that I'm not Hawkins or Feathers or what the hell. What do I do then – cosh her?'

'I haven't finished yet,' Royal said thinly. 'If you'll only listen. Once the dame is in the car you'll take off without delay, driving towards the east end of Second. When you reach the intersection at Glenmere Avenue slow the car and take Pete and Roy aboard. They'll look after the dame.'

Brad didn't like it much. Consideration of the whole picture brought a dryness to his mouth and a cold moisture to the palms of his hands. Still, you didn't earn two hundred and fifty grand knocking balls around a table in a pool hall. He hoped none of them noticed how he ran his tongue across his lips.

'I've got you this far, Jack. I get the dame into the car, pick up Pete and Roy at the intersection. Now I'm speeding for the east end of Second. What then?'

'You won't be speeding, pal. You'll keep your cool, no matter what. I've mapped out the streets you'll follow until you reach the suburbs. You'll hit the Frenchville highway at the upper turnoff. You'll keep to the highway as far as Bridgeport. You ought to make Bridgeport by nine-thirty or shortly afterwards. There you'll switch cars, getting into the one I'll be driving. Roy will turn the Caddy around and take it back to town. By then it will be almost ten, time for the Regan flunky to turn up at the Academy.'

'Sure. And you don't have to be told what he'll do as soon as he learns that another car called for the girl. His first reaction will be to call the cops.'

'No, he won't,' Royal argued. 'The first thing the flunky will do is get in touch with his boss. When he does I'll have already made contact with Regan and put the squeeze on him. Even if the driver should get in touch with the cops, the cops in turn will contact Regan, who will tell them that his daughter is okay and that there has been some mistake.'

'You're really banking on Regan having the presence of mind to hold his hand where the cops are concerned. But will he do so,

Jack? If he panics and raises the alarm we could be sunk.'

'You're the lad who can dream up the objections, aren't you, Brad?' Pete Kripp said in a low voice.

Brad looked at him again. He felt like getting up and kicking Kripp in the stomach. Royal made a gesture with a balled fist.

'Brad is right to make objections,' Royal said. 'And they aren't objections. He's simply putting forward possibilities.'

'So long as he doesn't start wishing for disaster. I knew a guy one time—'

'Shut up, Pete,' Royal said abruptly. 'Yeah, Brad, you have raised a point that bothered me. But I've studied all the angles and I'm certain I can tell how Regan's mind will operate. He'll listen to us all right. Still, if he does whistle the cops after us we'll have to scatter and pretty pronto.'

Brad didn't like this idea much either. Being involved to any degree in a kidnapping effort was inviting dire consequences if he were caught. But once again he had to weigh the risks against the reward that would be his for taking them if they won through. This was new ground to him and it made him uneasy, but he would learn to adjust his ideas and his outlook, just as he had done many times in the past.

'I get the picture,' he said presently. 'We hit Bridgeport and switch cars. You'll be driving then. If you'll be driving how can you put the call through to Regan at the appropriate time?'

'I'll be making the call,' Roy Judge told him. 'By the time you reach your destination I'll have a report ready to give Jack. Then we play it by ear from there.'

'Are you satisfied, Brad?'

'I guess so, Jack. They tell me you've got plenty of brains, and I just hope I wasn't getting false rumours.'

'Leave it to me,' Royal said brusquely.

'Where is our destination? If you're making for Bridgeport you're making for the hills. Have you got a suitable hideaway in there?'

Royal nodded. He didn't bother to enlarge or elaborate on what Brad had suggested.

'If Regan acts fast and sharp as I believe he will we won't have to hold the dame for long.'

'You know how you're going to have the money laid and how it's going to be collected?'

'Quit worrying, will you? This wasn't planned today or yesterday. We've been working on it for months.'

'I'm glad to hear it. Now, let's get back to the beginning once more. You talked about a plan of the streets you want me to follow. Can we get down to it now?'

'We'll get down to it now.'

'Another thing, Jack. I might want to show my face in Kentburg again. That doorman is going to remember what I looked like.'

'You'll wear a false moustache and dark glasses. That and the uniform you'll be wearing should take care of a disguise.'

'So there is a uniform. I can't wait to see what I look like in that.'

'Don't worry,' Kripp drawled at him. 'You'll still look as handsome as ever, pal.'

'Okay,' Royal growled. 'Knock off the monkey talk.' He took more stuff from the drawer and brought it over to a table. 'Come here, Brad and I'll show you,' he said.

Brad took his leave of the trio an hour later. He shut the room door behind him and went along the passage that would take him to the screen door and the back steps. He had almost gained the exit when Darla moved out of the living-room.

'Going already, Bradford?' she said.

'Yeah,' he told her. She had been taking on more gin and she was anything but steady on her pins. She stumbled or pretended to stumble and Brad caught her in his arms. 'Look out,' he said with a rough chuckle. 'You're just about pickled, sister.'

'What the hell else is there for a woman to do around this neck of the woods?' she complained thickly. She leaned heavily against him and her hand got jammed in at his stomach. She fumbled there and held her mouth up to him. 'What's wrong, Bradford? Have I lost that old magic touch I used to have?'

'You're sensational,' he said. 'But I've got to go.'

'Oh, yeah. You've got to go. Jack sent for you and you came running to see him. Now you're running away again. What is he plotting this time, Bradford?'

'You're way off. Nothing that I know of. Look, Darla, you shouldn't talk about Jack to folks. He wouldn't like it if you did. A guy has the right to his own business.'

She let out a gusty laugh and shifted her hand up to touch his mouth, patting it gently.

'Button up, button up! Don't give me that, buster. So okay. Let him mind his own business. Sure you won't come in for a drink?'

'Some other time, Darla. I've got to go.'

She shrugged and stepped back from him, her eyes disappointed and sullen.

'All right, mister. I can read the writing on the wall. I just don't have it any more, I guess.'

'Sure, you have it.'

He made himself put his arms about her waist and drew her towards him. She pressed hungrily in to him and plastered her lips against his. She really gave Brad a wild thrill before he remembered her brother and his cronies along there in that room. He pried himself loose, laughing thickly.

'Hey, wait. I don't want your big strong brother walloping the hide off me. Another time, Darla, huh?'

'Oh, all right,' she said with her mood changing quickly. 'I'm not throwing myself at you. Some of you guys make me sick.'

He left her hastily, going through the screen door and closing it behind him. The rain was sweeping in from the beach and he clattered down the stairway to reach his car. Driving back into town he discovered a lot of thoughts running in his head. Jack Royal was a fool for holding meetings of any kind in the proximity of his sister. Despite what Royal may or may not believe concerning Darla, she was anything but stable. If she decided to work out a grudge on him or anyone connected with him she would just go ahead and spill a bag of beans to the cops. Still, she was Jack's pigeon and his responsibility, and he had enough to occupy his mind right now without thinking of Darla.

The rain was easing off by the time he gained the suburbs of Kentburg and cruised on to his apartment building on Holbrook Street. He left his car in its customary niche at the side of the building and climbed the two flights of stairs to his quarters.

The door opened without having to use

his key and he knew with a little twinge of disappointment that Myrna was here. She lay on the couch in the living-room and tossed a magazine she had been reading to the floor on his entry.

'So you did come home after all? I've been here for hours in case you don't know.'

She was a tall girl, lissom and fair. She was wearing a blue dress that came to her knees and dipped at the bosom. At that moment the dress rode high about her tanned thighs but she made no move to adjust it.

'You didn't say you would be calling tonight. I was over on Denver, playing pool with some of the boys.'

'You sure you were doing just that?' she said coyly. 'Sure you weren't on the skedaddle after a little bit of hot-pants?'

'Cross my heart and hope to die,' Brad said with a forced grin. 'Look, I'll get you a drink and then we'll go out somewhere and dig up a meal.'

'Are you hungry then?' She patted the couch for him to come and sit beside her.

'Not very. Wait till I get us drinks.'

'All right, Brad, you do that. It's a stinking night outside and I had a meal before coming over. Let's just stay awhile and talk about old times.'

'If that's how you feel, honey.' He went into the kitchen to get a couple of cans of beer. Myrna was the one fly in the ointment, he felt. He would have to give her a tale of some description to put her off his trail for a few days. Indeed, he might have to ditch Myrna for keeps.

CHAPTER THREE

Next day he heard from Jack Royal around noon. Brad was going out to eat lunch when the phone in the hall rang. Artie Mullins from next door made it to the phone first and plucked up the receiver.

'Yes, you're in luck,' he said, looking at Brad. 'Yes, he's right here. Sure, sure. I'll put him on.' Artie looked at Brad with his moist eyes blinking. 'For you, Mr. Gilbert,' he cackled. 'You know something, I answer that damn thing nine times out of ten. You know something, the damn thing never rings for me. Nobody knows I'm alive.'

'Thanks, Artie.' Brad took the phone from the old man's fingers and waited until he tottered back into his room and closed the door. He spoke into the mouthpiece. 'Brad Gilbert.'

'This is me, Brad.' The voice belonged to Jack Royal. 'How's everything going with you.'

'Everything is going fine. Is that why you called?'

'Yeah, that's why,' Royal returned. 'Oh, about that party we were talking about, Brad. Make it here by no later than eight o'clock, will you?'

'Yeah,' Brad said slowly and frowned. 'I will. You already mentioned the time,' he added. 'Did you forget that?'

'No, I didn't,' Royal said with forced breeziness. 'I was sort of checking, Brad. Nothing more. Well, a man has been known to have had a change of heart after he's slept on a thing. We're only human, Brad.'

'Don't worry,' Brad said curtly. 'I said I would be there at eight and I'll be there at eight.'

'One point I should have advised you on. Leave your car at home, will you? Give yourself time to catch a cab. We don't want to clutter up the place.'

Brad was on the verge of objecting to this but he refrained from doing so. Jack Royal was the boss and whatever Royal said went without question.

'I get you,' he said and hung up.

He spent the afternoon in his old haunts on Denver Avenue. From the pool hall to Gilly's Bar. From Gilly's Bar to the pool hall. He found pool very relaxing and was able to forget about things when he was playing a good game.

He had told Myrna he was after a new job with a trucking company and he might be out of town for a day or so as a consequence, so that she didn't have to be disappointed if she visited and he wasn't at home. Myrna had stayed at the apartment overnight and left early this morning to catch a bus to the midtown department store where she was employed as a sales clerk. She had swallowed his story and evinced no suspicion.

He had the growing conviction that it really might be best to ditch the girl if the trick he had committed himself to paid off. It wouldn't create a stir if he should vanish out of town, but if he brought the dame along her friends might commence asking questions after a while, and her employers could be tempted to alarm the cops.

At nine o'clock Brad was sitting in his car at the front of the Art Academy on Second Avenue. The Academy ran classes on every night of the week except Saturday and Sunday, and from where he sat he was able to make out the doorman in his cubicle. He was middle-aged and wore glasses, and he was holding a book he was reading within inches of his nose. With vision like that he wasn't going to mark many details of the chauffeur who spoke to him tomorrow night.

Brad moved off at a few minutes past nine on the route laid down by Royal. There were no traffic lights at the Glenmere Avenue intersection, but traffic tended to slow up there all the same, so that no one would pay much attention when he eased off for Pete and Roy.

Street by street he went though Jack Royal's instructions, and was amazed at the sparseness of traffic on these thoroughfares. It gave him a little more confidence in Royal and when eventually he arrived at Bridgeport his wristwatch said nine-thirty on the dot. Royal had made dry runs also.

At the village Brad was tempted to turn off into the hills, but then he realised it was unnecessary as Royal would be driving for the rest of the way. There were hundreds of roads and tracks up there, but Royal would know exactly where he was going.

He turned in early that night and slept late the next morning. He didn't move out of the apartment except to eat, in case Royal would decide to contact him with last-minute instructions.

As the day advanced he became aware of a growing nervousness, but it stemmed more from anticipation than from fear, he told himself. He knew the sensation too well, or had known it in those steaming jungles in Vietnam. Waiting for the action to begin was worse than the action itself. You found yourself getting tense and jittery, but once the ball opened you went in there weaving and there was no time left to analyse your psyche.

At six o'clock he heard the phone ringing in the hall but kept himself from going to answer it. He heard old Artie shuffling from his room and heard Artie talking dimly to the caller. Then his door was thumped and Brad jumped. What the hell. What the blue merry hell.

He calmed himself. He was behaving like a hen that had just given birth to a duck's egg. He opened the door and Artie was blinking at him, blinking and grinning widely.

'You're wanted, Mr. Gilbert. Some young lady on the line. You know something, I never–'

'Yeah, okay, Artie.' He brushed the old man aside and lifted the dangling receiver. 'Is that you, Brad?' Myrna said. 'I feel horrible this evening, Brad. There's a good movie on at the Palace, and I wondered–'

'Sorry,' he cut in on the girl. He spoke too sharply, he supposed, but he had made everything perfectly clear to her last night. 'I wish I could, doll,' he added hastily. 'But that job I'm going after ... I'm seeing a guy later this evening. This guy knows somebody who–'

'Who knows somebody,' the girl cut in on him in turn. 'Oh, all right, Brad. Look, the truth is I hate the feeling of you going out of town at all.' She laughed. 'It's crazy, isn't it?'

'It isn't for ever,' he said on a lighter note. 'And it sure is good to feel wanted. Well, thanks for calling, Myrna. Find a pal and go to the Palace anyhow, huh?'

'Bye, Brad. Don't be gone for long.'

'I won't. So long, honey.' He hung up.

Talking with Myrna had cut through his tension and now he wasn't so keenly on edge. Even so, he thought the next hour and a half dragged by on feet of lead.

Before leaving the apartment he dug out a .38 Police Positive from the bottom of his suitcase and checked it prior to pushing it away in his jacket pocket. Royal hadn't mentioned anything about weapons, but Brad failed to see why he shouldn't fit himself out with a measure of insurance.

He walked to the end of the Street and caught a cab, telling the driver to take him to Swift's Beach. He reached the Beach with five minutes on hand, paid off the cabbie and walked round the amusement concessions to strike the path leading to Darla Grant's house.

He saw the big Cadillac parked back in the shadows. It would be a stolen car, he was sure, as Royal would hardly have rented it. He didn't have to worry whether it was stolen or rented. He would get his turn out of it and then Judge would take over.

It was a clear night, he realised as he mounted the back steps. A soft breeze was blowing in from the sea, but there was no sign of clouds anywhere. It didn't matter what kind of night it was, but he wouldn't have minded rain, as then it would have lent a blurring effect and lessened the likelihood of anyone paying too much attention to him.

Jack Royal opened the door to his brisk rap. Royal looked relieved at sight of him, Brad thought, and wondered if he'd imagined he would back out of the deal at the last minute.

'Are you on your own?' he asked the squat man when he had led him along the passage to his room.

'On my own,' Royal grunted with a faint grin. 'You don't have to worry about Darla either. She's gone out some place.'

That was a real relief. Brad told himself. He was in no mood for coping with the woman tonight.

Royal showed him a uniform he had dug up from somewhere. It seemed more like a cinema commissionaire's outfit, but he guessed it would do.

'I hope it fits.'

'It'll fit well enough. Pull it on and we'll see how it looks. I got it from one of those Hire-A-Suit joints. Then try this moustache for size as well.'

Royal stood over him while he stripped and folded his clothes. He frowned and pointed at the gun.

'What are you going to do with that?'

'It's my lucky charm, Jack. It goes everywhere I go. You have some objection?'

'Just keep it out of sight, that's all.'

The uniform was somewhat on the tight side but it would get him by in a pinch. Royal made him sit down and applied spirit gum to his upper lip, then pressed the moustache in place. Next he handed Brad a pair of sunglasses.

'Put them on and stand up.' He chuckled throatily when Brad did so. 'Your own mother wouldn't recognize you now.'

Brad snapped the sunglasses off and put them in a pocket of the tunic. He asked Royal for a sheet of wrapping paper, or for any kind of paper.

You want to wrap your clothes?'

'I want to take them with me. I don't want to have to spend more time than's necessary in this gear.'

A few moments later Brad, with his jacket and trousers bundled under his arm, was ready to go down to the Cadillac. Jack Royal went down with him and saw him seated in the car.

'Don't forget the glasses, Brad. They make the disguise complete.'

'Does the Regan chauffeur wear sunglasses?'

'He could if he developed eyestrain. It's time to go, Brad.'

'Yeah,' Brad said. There was a queer little fluttering of excitement in his veins as he looked at Royal. 'You'll see us at Bridgeport?'

'I'll see you there. And quit worrying, will

you. All you have to do is get the dame out of the Academy and into the car. Pete and Roy will take over at the intersection. You can't go wrong, Brad.'

'I'm not going to go wrong, Jack,' Brad rejoined coolly. 'Be seeing you, friend.'

He switched on the engine and the big car purred away. Jack Royal watched it until it was lost to his sight, then he hurried up the back steps to the frame building.

In the room that he used as an office Royal sat down by the telephone, lifted the receiver and dialled. In a moment he heard Roy Judge's voice at the other end of the line.

'All systems go, Roy. He's on his way.'

'Got you,' Judge said and hung up.

Royal had a quick drink, lit a cigarette and then prepared to leave the house.

'All right, Carol, that will do for now. You're coming along wonderfully, my dear. If you continue to improve as you're doing at the moment there's the chance that I might fit you into a niche in Ray Goetz's next production. He has asked me for two girls, at least.'

'Thank you, Miss Bridges,' Carol said to the horsy-looking woman in the ridiculous black tights. She moved off the stage to the wall where Lin Dorsey and Jim Leasor were sweating it out, awaiting their scene to be staged.

44

Jim supplied her with a cigarette and a light, and Lin began telling her what a fortunate girl she was.

'If only I could get a break like that, Carol. Just one tiny break in a real theatre. I wish I knew what the heck it is I do wrong that displeases Miss Bridges so much.'

Lin Dorsey was a slim, delicately-constructed redhead. She had enrolled at the Academy a few weeks after Carol had made her decision to do so. It wasn't that Carol had any genuine ambitions to be a star and to see her name in lights. One of her friends had been taking lessons, and at the time it seemed like another good excuse to get away from Seaway Heights for a couple of hours.

Now Carol was becoming slightly bored with the whole idea. It was all very well for Lin and Jim and Beaulah and the dozen other young men and women who had been smitten by the acting bug. Their means were limited and they saw the end result as a good way to make a living. She didn't have to work for a living if she didn't want to. Even if she did get a part in a new Ray Goetz production it wouldn't do anything startling for her. She enjoyed acting to a certain extent but she certainly didn't see herself becoming dedicated to it.

She liked the company here, the pseudo-bohemian atmosphere. But she liked the

45

company and the atmosphere of the artists' colony just as well. In short she welcomed any diversion from the dull, wrapped-in-cotton existence that her father willed on her.

If only she had the guts to pack her bags and run away. If she did this she would find excitement in plenty, she would have the opportunity of sampling life in the raw. At this stage in her dreamings reservations would insinuate themselves, doubts, small niggling fears. She had never known what it was to be without money, to be without servants tripping over her at every turn. She might not care for such a drastic extreme as she often contemplated. She might not be equipped for it, mentally or physically. Of course she would have to have money to get by with. Everyone needed money to get by with.

Then there was marriage. Marriage offered an escape, and Dick Knight had offered her marriage. But her father disapproved of Dick and considered he would fail to make a suitable partner for her. He tolerated Dick for no better reason than to humour her. She would grow away from him eventually, find a young man on her own social level, a young man who could look after her as she was accustomed to being looked after.

Occasionally Carol wished that her father might die. It was a private thought that she harboured in her subconscious. She never really willed it to surface and tantalise her, but it did, readily and often. With her father gone she would come into his estate. She could live as she wanted to live and have her bohemian friends around her from morning to night. There would be no one to object to this and frown on that. She could get back to driving her car, going where she wanted to go, doing exactly as she pleased.

She always stifled this thought immediately. It was evil, and its pettiness belied her strong, outgoing personality. And she did love her father. He might be the next thing to a tyrant, but if he ruled her existence with an iron hand he believed he was doing it for her own good. He had lost her mother in an accident and it had done something dreadful to him. He had grown more possessive with every day that had gone by since the accident. Then the accident she had suffered herself had put the lid on it. After that he could scarcely let her out of his sight.

Miss Bridges was directing a scene from a Tennesse Williams play. Beaulah Coates and Stanley Trask were playing the parts, and all of the other students were paying the closest attention. Jim Leasor had his knee up against hers. When she glanced at him he winked and increased the pressure of his knee a trifle.

'I really go for this bit,' he said with his

broad smile. 'And you must give Miss Bridges credit for her willingness to experiment to the hilt.'

Carol didn't answer him. She looked at her wristwatch and saw that the time was five minutes to nine. Another hour of this to go and then Sam Travis would be calling for her.

She was brooding about Dick Knight when she noticed the door at the far end of the large hall opening. Frank Burley stepped through the doorway and signalled. Carol looked at Jim and Lin on either side of her. Jim had spotted old Frank too and frowned.

'Who, me?' he mouthed.

'I think he wants me,' Carol said.

'I'll find out,' Jim told her and tip-toed towards the doorman. He hurried back and Carol noticed that his face had paled. 'He wants you, Carol. I'll get your coat.'

With her coat in hand Carol made her way to the end of the hall, puzzled as to what was going on.

'Is something the matter, Frank?'

'I'm afraid so, Miss Regan. Your father's chauffeur is outside. Your father is ill and he wants you home at once.

'What!'

Carol ran out to the street, seeing the Cadillac parked at the curb, the engine running, Sam Travis sitting at the wheel.

Frank Burley dashed out after her and

opened the rear door for her when Travis continued to sit where he was. Travis usually stood to attention and opened the door for her, and the fact that he was so eager to get away proved that her father's condition must be serious.

She slid on to the seat and Burley slammed the door. He stood back and signalled the driver. There wasn't any need for this, as the big car leaped forward at once and swung out into the traffic stream.

'What is it, Sam?' she panted at the driver. 'Is Dad really ill? Did he have a stroke... Sam, why are you wearing those glasses?'

'Take it easy, Miss Regan.'

That voice, Carol thought wildly, it doesn't belong to Sam Travis at all!

'Hey, wait,' she cried. 'If you aren't Sam Travis, then who are you? What is going on? Where are you taking me?'

'Home, Miss Regan. Please be calm.'

Calm! Carol sank back on her seat and stared at him. It was crazy, but there must be some logical answer to it. Perhaps her father had fired Sam and taken on a new driver. But since Travis had left her off at the Academy earlier? That was impossible.

The car slowed down at an intersection. Carol had a brief impression of two men darting through the traffic towards it. Horns blasted. One of the men missed the fender of a Lincoln Continental by inches. The rear door opened and the two men piled in, throwing Carol into a paroxysm of fear.

'Take it easy, sister,' Roy Judge urged calmly. 'Don't make a riot and you'll be sweet okay.'

CHAPTER FOUR

Brad had come out in a cold sweat. It was pasted like chill gummy water to the palms of his hands, to his forehead, to the knotted planes of his jaws. Holy hell, he thought bitterly, amazed and disappointed with himself, he had imagined there were more guts under his belt than this. There was a sick void where his stomach ought to be; his tongue clove thickly to the roof of his mouth. Even in Vietnam he had never experienced a sensation like this. It wasn't really fear, he discovered, when he took a moment to analyse it. It was some kind of powerful disgust, revulsion. When you had a fight on your hands then you fought, but you couldn't call this a fight unless you considered it a battle with yourself, a struggle to throttle your conscience and forget your codes of conduct. He didn't want to kidnap anybody; he certainly didn't want to abduct a helpless girl who didn't have the strength nor the opportunity to retaliate.

Grimly he attempted to banish these thoughts from his mind. If he weakened and allowed them to dominate him he would angle the car in to the sidewalk and yell cop at the top of his voice.

Somehow he secured a measure of calm and reason. If he backed out of the deal at this late stage he was done. No matter where he went or how he tried to hide himself, Jack Royal would find him, would seek him out and kill him. He had heard stories of Royal's potential, of his capabilities. And what about that two hundred and fifty grand? Did he not need it any more?

Yes, he did need it. He did have the equipment to go through with what he had to do. It wasn't as if they were going to kill the dame, or even molest her. It wasn't as if they were going to keep her away from her home and her father for any length of time. So what? So okay. Simmer down. Think about the percentage instead. Think of lying in the sun and lighting fat cigars with dollar bills.

He was clear of the town when he dared glance back at the rear. There had been a hectic struggle back there. He had heard it, the writhings and strugglings and gruntings. He had heard the girl whimper but he pretended it was happening elsewhere. Now she was still between Kripp and Judge. They had taped her mouth and her eyes, and her arms appeared to be fastened behind her. They had dragged her down below the level of the windows. He wondered if they had socked her to render her unconscious.

He stabbed his foot at the gas pedal.

'What do you figure you're doing?' Roy Judge demanded presently. 'Warming up for the Indianapolis?'

'Leave me alone, Roy.'

'Slow down, you goof,' Kripp snarled. 'If you don't you're going to have a bunch of speedcops on our tail.'

Brad released the pressure. They were on the highway now and surging towards Bridgeport. He exerted control on his breathing, forcing the air in and out of his lungs. The moisture began to evaporate from his forehead and the palms of his hand. Exhilaration superseded the sickening, gnawing dismay. They had taken the first and most formidable hurdle in their stride; there were a few others ahead, but there shouldn't be too many. And soon they would be cantering along the home straight.

He calmed, thought clearly and coolly. He drove expertly and surrendered nothing of caution and care.

They were a quarter mile from the village when Roy Judge touched his arm with his knuckles.

'Slow off, Brad.'

He slowed obediently, gauging what was coming next.

'There's a hard shoulder fifty or sixty yards along,' Judge told him. 'There ought to be a car parked.'

The car was parked. Brad spotted the red

rear lights and aimed the Cadillac in to them. He switched off the engine, set the parking brake and alighted. Jack Royal appeared in the gloom.

'How did it go?' he said hoarsely.

'Like a dream,' Brad replied. He felt as though he had just emerged from a successful foray, not only in one piece but without a scratch into the bargain. He snatched off the uniform cap and flung it into the Caddy.

'Take that out,' Royal snarled. 'Leave nothing.'

'Don't burn your beard, Jack.'

It surprised him to see that the girl was conscious. Kripp took her shoulders and Judge grabbed her legs. Her skirts were up somewhere around her waist. He saw smooth, curved limbs. She began wriggling frantically like a freshly-caught trout. It was a moment's work to transfer her to the rear seat of Royal's car.

'Get in at the back,' Royal ordered him. He was obeying when he remembered the bundle of clothes. He went to the Cadillac, snatched out the bundle and then took over from Judge. The girl lunged against him as he flopped on to the seat.

'I'm gonna thump you if you don't quit it, baby,' Kripp growled throatily.

'You're not going to touch her, Pete.'

The girl subsided as though she derived comfort from hearing him say it. Royal slammed beneath the wheel and the car spun into motion, heading on towards the village and the hills. Brad looked out of the window and saw Roy turning the Cadillac.

Judge checked his strapwatch by the dash light and noted that the time was now nine thirty-five. In twenty-five minutes the Regan chauffeur would be drawing up at the front of the Art Academy. After that it was anybody's guess what might happen.

It wasn't as though he, Jack and Pete hadn't explored all the angles, because they had. He had wanted to ask Brad to give him the precise details of his encounter with the doorman and his reactions, but Jack's instructions were that nothing was discussed in the hearing of the girl. Roy failed to see how this would signify one thing or another to the girl, but what Jack said went and nobody argued over it.

As Judge viewed it now and as they had viewed it collectively before, when the doorman got Brad's message of Wesley Regan's illness and transmitted it to the girl, he might also tell the old bird who managed the Academy, and the old bird might just take it into her head to put a phone call through to the big house on Seaway Heights. If this happened then Wesley Regan would smell a rat and might already have taken some kind of action.

It wouldn't matter that much, Judge told himself. They had got the dame and she was on her way to the roost in the hills. Regan might have lost his head and rung in to the cops, but when he got the message he could tell the cops he had jumped the gun and his daughter was really okay.

All the same, Judge was curious to know what had actually taken place. He trod hard on the accelerator.

He left the Cadillac in a midtown parking area. He spent three minutes in wiping the steering wheel and the dash and then the seats. Satisfied, he left the car, the keys in his pocket, and walked smartly round a corner where he picked up his own car. By now the time was eight minutes before ten.

He drove fast but carefully to Second Avenue and hauled up on the side of the street opposite the Art Academy. His heart skipped a beat when he spotted the big Caddy at the front of the joint.

The chauffeur was out of the car and Judge watched the entrance until two men appeared, both in uniform – the doorman and the Regan flunky. They talked for a few minutes and the chauffeur moved on to the sidewalk to stare up and down the street. Then he and the doorman went into another huddle, and finally the chauffeur hurried to the Caddy and slid in behind the wheel.

Judge saw him pick up an instrument and

hold it to his mouth and ear. A telephone. He waited no longer, but drove away slowly and on out of Second. So far the trick was going like a smooth song.

Judge braked at a phone booth on First, alighted and shut himself in the booth. He gathered up the receiver and dialled the Regan number. He had a reply practically at once, a hoarse, rasping croak.

'Carol, is it you?'

'It isn't Carol, Mr. Regan,' Judge said. 'Listen to me and listen real good. Carol is okay. She'll be home very soon. Providing you don't do anything silly such as calling for the cops. Have you already called the cops, Regan?'

'No, no! What the hell is this? Where is Carol? Who in blue blazes are you...'

'It's a snatch,' Judge told him bluntly. 'Just a snatch. I want a million bucks in hundreds. The numbers have got to be mixed and mixed plenty. They will not be marked in any way whatever. Have you got all that?'

'You mean you've kidnapped her?' Wesley Regan roared. 'But you can't do this to me. Do you hear me, you goddam bastard, you can't do this to me!'

'Okay,' Judge said coldly. 'If that's how you want it...'

'No, wait...' He heard Regan moaning to himself. When he spoke again his voice sounded thin and weary. 'All right. I'll do it.

57

Do you understand that? I'll do it. Tell me where you want the money brought and I'll take it there myself.'

'When?'

'Now! I'll get my banker out. I'll do anything to protect my girl.'

'Not now, Regan. Cool off. Take it easy. She's safe and she'll remain safe. So long as you don't do anything silly. I'll call you in the morning.'

'No. Don't hang up! Wait...'

Judge broke the connection and smiled to himself. Things were going pretty well, he thought. So far Wesley Regan hadn't put in an alarm to the police, and by the sound of him just now it was the very last thing he would consider while there was hope of his daughter being safe and sound and her early return being imminent.

Judge left the phone booth and drove around for a while before finishing up in a bar where he drank two highballs. It was a strange bar to him and he knew none of the customers, which was the way he wanted it right then.

At ten-thirty he went into the phone booth and dialed another number. Now he had Jack Royal on the other end of the line. This occasioned Judge great relief also, as it meant that the party had reached their destination without incident.

'What d'you know,' he said with his neighing laugh. 'You're one guy whose brains I admire.'

'Never mind the fluff,' Royal retorted. 'How did it go at your end?'

'Nothing could be better,' Judge responded carelessly, flipping a cigarette to his lips and lighting it. 'The Caddy turned up at the joint on schedule. I found a spot where I could watch what was taking place. There must have been some fuss. A little later I had a word with our friend on the phone. He agrees completely with the whole idea. Marvellous, isn't it?'

'Not bad,' Jack Royal murmured. He sounded a trifle nervous, Judge imagined, and was trying to cover it up. But no, he was wrong, Judge reflected immediately, there was nothing nervy about Royal. 'I'll hear from you in the morning,' he added, wanting to get off the line.

'Sure thing. Be seeing you.'

Judge left the booth and had another few drinks. He came out of the bar an hour later and drove to the cheap hotel on the north side where he had a room. He collected his key and went up to the third floor in the automatic elevator. Ten minutes later he was in bed and five minutes after that he was sound asleep.

Judge awakened at eight next morning, washed and shaved and called room service to send up a breakfast consisting of fruit juice, toast, scrambled eggs and black coffee.

'Are the papers on the newsstand yet?' he asked.

'Yes, sir. They're delivered promptly at seven.'

'Bring me the *Kentburg Gazette* and the *Times,* will you?'

'Certainly, Mr. Judge.'

He went through the two papers while he wolfed his breakfast. There was no mention of the Regan kidnapping in either of the papers. He hadn't expected that there would be. Even if old Wesley had gone to the cops the cops would see to it that the snatch was kept a close secret for the time being.

At eight-thirty Judge left the hotel and walked two blocks to a pay phone. Shutting himself in the box he dialled the Regan house once more. A woman took the call, a maid, he guessed.

'I'd like to speak to Mr. Regan, please,' Judge said in a mild, apologetic voice.

'Is that you, Dick?'

Judge frowned and said no, he wasn't Dick. Would she mind getting Mr. Regan on the line.

A minute afterwards the millionaire was breathing heavily into his ear.

'Yes, I'm here!' he said in a tight, strained whisper. 'What is it? Are you–'

'Listen, chum, I thought I told you not to

try contacting the cops.'

'What! But – but I didn't. I swear to you that I didn't. Do you think I'm mad? Look, I promise you faithfully that I didn't–'

'Okay,' Judge broke in on him. 'Let it ride. But remember, boss, on the very minute that you take anyone into your confidence, and I do mean anyone, it will be too bad for the dame.'

'Where is she? I said I would pay you, didn't I? Make whatever arrangements that suit you and I'll do exactly as you say.'

'That's being smart. Have you been in touch with your banker?'

'I rang him first thing this morning. I'll have the money in my possession within the next hour.'

'Good. But watch what you tell your banker. I'll be in touch with you later. Just sit tight.'

Wesley Regan was babbling something when he hung up.

Judge continued his walk to another booth and dialed the house in the hills. It was Peter Kripp who answered the phone and he brought Jack Royal in short order.

'The papers are clean. I gave our friend a further shot in the arm. He's to have what we want inside the next hour.'

'You don't think he has been talkative?'

'Not by the sound of him.'

'Okay. You'd better get up here now.'

'I'm on my way,' Judge told him and broke the connection.

He walked back to his hotel, enjoying the bright morning and the feel of the warm sun on his face. It was almost as easy as falling off a log. He wondered what he would do with his share of the loot. Jack said they would all have to split and clear and forget they had ever met. That was okay with him. It was the big break he had been searching for all his life. Now it had happened. He could scarcely believe it. But wait, he told himself, don't start counting those beautiful little chickens until they are properly hatched.

Judge didn't enter the hotel again, but got into his car on the hotel parking area and drove to the outskirts of Kentburg. He stopped at a gas station short of the highway, tanked up and had the oil level checked, then he settled back behind the wheel and drove at a leisurely speed for Bridgeport and the turnoff into the hills.

Wesley Regan sat in his big, luxuriously furnished study and stared at the bright red telephone on his desk. He was a tall, heavily-built man in his early sixties, with good features that had once been clean-cut and rugged but which were now getting too full and flaccid.

Regan's thick fingers drummed on the desk as he continued to stare at the phone.

Indecision combined with worry grooved deep lines on his forehead. He had swallowed his anger in an effort to think calmly and logically.

All he had to do was lift that phone again and dial police headquarters. In a matter of minutes he would have the finest police brains at his disposal. The idea was tempting, unbearably tempting. How many times in the past had he been let down by the police when he had need of them? Never. He had always found them courteous, efficient and utterly reliable. Well then, what was holding him now? Did he not trust in them any more? Was he frightened that somehow or other it would leak out that he had requested them to find his kidnapped daughter?

'Yes, I'm frightened,' he muttered hoarsely. 'I'm as frightened as hell. Carol is worth a million to me. Carol is worth every damn penny I have. I would give my life for her were it necessary. My own life...'

A tear rose to his eye and he blinked it away furiously. He pulled over the phone and rang Marvin Biersby again.

'This is Regan,' he said gruffly when Biersby came on. 'Will your messenger be much longer?'

'I'm doing my best, Mr. Regan,' Biersby replied in his oily tone. 'It is a lot of money, Mr. Regan. If it didn't have to be in hundreds I could manage a lot quicker.'

'It's got to be in hundreds, Marvin. Exactly as I told you. And don't forget what else I told you. No gossiping. If you mention my business to anybody I'll have your guts for suspenders.'

Biersby laughed weakly.

'Don't worry, Mr. Regan. As I said, I'm doing my best. The trouble is, too, finding my guards at this hour of the morning.'

'You find them,' Regan growled. 'And do it fast, Marvin.'

He slammed down the phone and took a fat cigar from a box at his hand. He sat smoking for a long time, smoking and drumming his fingers on the desk. He looked idly through the window at the trim lawns shining like emerald under the new sun. Lorne Keller was busy on his mower, sitting on it as though he were in the cockpit of a tank. The mower thrummed quietly. The smell of the grass cuttings drifted through the open window.

The ringing of the phone caused Regan to jump.

'Yeah?' he said in a strained voice when he grabbed the receiver. 'Wes Regan here.'

'Sorry if I'm disturbing you, Mr. Regan,' the voice at the other end said. 'I was hoping to speak with Carol.'

Regan's eyes narrowed in a tight frown. Damn it to hell. He had overlooked the danger that Dick Knight could pose.

'Oh, hello, Dick... It's you. Carol isn't up yet. But look, she was talking last night of going out somewhere this morning. You can see her later, huh?'

'Very well, Mr. Regan, but–'

'I'm busy, Dick. Sorry. I'll tell her to call you. Okay?'

Regan hung up and puffed worriedly at his cigar.

CHAPTER FIVE

Brad Gilbert grunted in his sleep, rolled over, and opened his eyes. He had been having a bad dream, a dream in which he was driving the Cadillac. The blonde Carol Regan was on the front seat beside him, clawing at his sleeve and screaming into his ear.

'Stop! If you don't stop they're going to kill you. It's your last chance to stop and save yourself.'

Behind them were a bunch of prowl cars, sirens raging, headlamps pinning them down in the dark maw of the woods like a blinded, helpless butterfly. He had crushed the Cadillac against a tree when he awoke.

He lay there, shivering, willing the remnants of the nightmare to fade before the reality of morning. But was the reality in any manner preferable to the nightmare? Where did reality fizzle out and the nightmare begin? Where did the nightmare end and he was free and alone with a quarter million bucks in a suitcase to spend?

He shook himself. He told himself he'd better get a firm hand on his thinking and pull himself together. He was committed now and there was no way he could get out of it. The only thing he could do was make the best of what was here and what he had, his resources of humour and courage, his readiness to take each day as it dawned, and to sleep content when the sun was wrapped up for the night.

The sun was filtering through the flimsy window curtains, and when Brad listened to what was around him instead of to his own thoughts, he heard birds singing and chirruping up there in the piney woods. The piney woods were all about them. Over the front bench and on down the undergrowth-cluttered slope were the waters of Pine Lake.

That was what the locality was called. Pine Lake Enterprises. The Enterprises were a cluster of widely scattered summer residences owned by a syndicate in Los Angeles. Jack Royal had told him all about it last night. He had rented the cabin – it was little better than a glorified cabin, part brick, part hand-hewn logs, with electricity and a telephone thrown in and water piped from a spring higher up in the hills – three weeks ago in preparation for the consummation of his plans. He had rented it as Jack Wade with a bogus address in Kingston. Nobody would ever bother to query the validity of the name and address he had tendered, he had explained to Brad. True, there were always people coming and going to and from the other cabins in the vicinity, but they were spaced far apart so that there was little probability of neighbours dropping in to borrow coffee.

Last night he and Pete Kripp had taken turns in guarding his back room in the west wing where Carol Regan was quartered. It was a room with strong walls, a strong door, and a small high window that would give a rattlesnake bother negotiating. Brad had taken the first portion of the night and Kripp had taken the latter.

The only thing that Royal had overlooked was storing in a supply of food, but he said he believed there was a sort of general store up on the main road where they could get what they required to tide them over.

Brad yawned and stretched himself. Then he rose and went to the window to peer out. In the darkness last night it had been impossible to get a clear picture of the locality. A brief description from Royal had had to suffice.

The view from the window was of trees, an almost impenetrable wall of them. He saw a few birch, lots of pine. There were plenty of huckleberry bushes, sumac, wild azalea and laurel. By craning his neck he could see the tail-end of Jack Royal's big Packard.

He pulled on his trousers, left the room and went round a corner to a corridor leading to the bathroom. Pete Kripp was sitting on a stool, hat to the crown of his head, blear-eyed and yawning.

'Where are you going?' he scowled at Brad.

'Where do you think I'm going? It's a free country. There's a john and running water, isn't there?'

'She's there,' Kripp informed him sleepily and jerked his thumb to the direction of the bathroom door.

Brad gulped and felt a flutter in the region of his stomach.

'The dame?'

'That's right,' Kripp sneered. 'The dame. We do have one living with us, you know.'

'Okay, okay. Don't get steamed. Is it all right to let her use the bathroom? I mean, she couldn't get out?'

'She can't get out. Go stew yourself for a while. Jack has gone to find the store. When he gets back I'm gonna turn in. You've got a long day ahead of you, buster.'

Brad was about to return to his bedroom when the lock on the bathroom door clicked and the girl emerged. He would have beaten a retreat anyhow if it wasn't for the fact that she was already staring at him.

She was wearing the pink and black dress she had been wearing last night and had her coat draped about her shoulders. Her wealth of blonde hair was brushed out about her neck and shoulders in a cloud of burnished gold. She had a strong-featured face, a long nose and squarish chin – strong features but essentially feminine. The eyes that held Brad's coldly were a deep hazel shade. They struggled with him for a long moment before dropping.

'Is this where the fun stops and the serious stuff begins?' she jolted Brad by saying.

He fought with a dry mouth to form words.

'Quit worrying,' he said gruffly. 'Nobody's going to touch you.'

'That's something to cheer about, I guess.'

Kripp let her past him and winked broadly at Brad before he followed her closely to her room. He heard the room door bang and let out his breath in a long whistling sigh. Bolts rattled home.

Royal got back to the cabin at just before nine. He had sacks of groceries with him and looked hot and bothered.

'I should have taken the damn car,' he grumbled. 'It's almost a mile to that general store.'

'Still, it was worth it,' Brad grinned. 'What did you get to eat, Jack?' He poked in the sacks and turned up his nose. 'You sure it was a general store and not a cannery?'

'It'll keep us eating, won't it?'

'Sure it will. But what about that girl? She's bound to have a cultivated lining to her stomach.'

'If she turns snooty at the grub we serve her she can starve,' was the short rejoinder. 'There's eggs and ham. Some cans of juice. Syrup. Wheatcakes. I think I did pretty well.'

'So you did, Jack. I hope it's you does the cooking back home and not Darla.'

Royal lit a cigarette and stared glumly at the phone.

'I told that punk to ring me by nine at the outside,' he said, consulting his watch. 'What do you make it?'

'Nine on the button.'

'Did you listen to any news on the radio?'

'I've just got up.'

Brad and Royal were in the kitchen with the gas stove burning when the phone jangled. By the time they reached the living-room Pete Kripp was answering it.

'Hello, Roy. Yes, he's here—'

'Give me that,' Royal said and snatched the receiver from the sallow-faced man. 'Go ahead, Roy.'

The papers were clean, Judge told him. He had just given Regan his second shot in the arm.

'You don't think he has been talkative?'

'Not by the sound of him.'

'Okay. You'd better get up here now.'

'I'm on my way.'

There was a faint smile on Royal's broad features as he replaced the receiver on its rest. Suddenly his eyes narrowed on Kripp.

71

'Is that door locked?'

'Sure, it's locked.'

'Well, go stay there just in case. There's nothing in the papers. Roy gave daddy another squeeze. He thinks he's falling in line with our plan.'

Kripp went back to the girl's bedroom door and Brad and Royal returned to the kitchen. Royal was quite an expert at cooking, Brad noted. Perhaps he had to be when he lived with Darla. Darla hadn't struck Brad as the ideal domestic type.

He reverted to the business on hand.

'How are you going to make the lift?' he asked the squat man. This would be the second most dangerous aspect of the scheme, and he wondered exactly how it would take place.

'I've got it figured,' Royal said shortly. 'I'm going to let the old coot worry for a while.'

'You're what?' Brad choked. 'But that's just crazy, Jack. The longer you keep him on the hook the more risks we're going to have to run. How can you depend on him? How do you know he won't change his mind – or panic – and call in the cops?'

'Stop beefing, Brad,' the other said quietly. 'I've done all the thinking up to now, haven't I? We've got this far. So okay, we'll travel the rest of the way.'

If he imagined this would satisfy Brad he was wrong. Brad hadn't gambled on any long-term project. He wanted the whole gag over and done with in the shortest possible time. To his way of reckoning, the longer they held the girl the more likely they were to run foul of the cops.

'I just hope you know what you're doing, Jack.'

'I know what I'm doing. Here, grab some of this food and then take breakfast to the dame.'

Brad was reluctant to face the girl but he was just as reluctant to keep turning on Royal. There was too much money involved, he concluded. He wasn't supposed to do the thinking or the planning: they trusted Royal to do this. If he thought it best to keep the girl's father on the hook then let him keep him on the hook.

Kripp moved into the kitchen to eat as Brad headed for the girl's bedroom with the loaded tray.

'Just watch,' Kripp said. 'She won't let you in there. She's got more spunk than I figured a pampered doll would have.'

'So you tried to get in, huh?'

'Don't be silly.' Dark colour entered Knipp's sallow cheeks and Brad had to swallow a surge of anger.

Royal had fixed up the room door with two bolts in preparation for its being utilised for this purpose, so that Brad had to place the tray on the floor until he released the bolts. Then he lifted the tray and tapped the door with the toe of his shoe.

The door opened an inch and he found himself being skewered with the hazel eyes.

'What is it?' she said icily.

'What does it smell like?' he said with a forced grin. 'Your breakfast.'

'Take it away. I don't want it.'

She was contriving a situation that he didn't feel adequate to cope with. He affected an ugly sneer.

'Please yourself. If you don't eat you'll weaken and then you'll be less troublesome to handle.' He turned slightly to lay the tray down preparatory to bolting the door.

'No, wait,' she said. 'I will take it.'

'Please make up your mind, baby.'

She opened the door wide enough for him to enter. Recalling what Pete Kripp had said, he suspected a trick.

'Back off, lady,' he ordered in a brusque tone.

She retreated into the room and Brad entered, closing the door behind him with his heel. The room was furnished with a bed, a small dressing table, two chairs and a coffee table. There was a square of grey carpet on the floor. Brad noticed that there had been a sizeable window in the wall but it had been bricked in and papered over. The small high window permitted very little light to trickle through. It gave the room the atmosphere of a prison cell.

He laid the tray on the coffee table and stepped back to the door.

'What's your hurry?'

He stared at her, a quick thrill rippling along his nerves.

Kripp was right and she did have more spunk than was to be expected from her. She drew one of the chairs up to the table and sat down, helping herself to a drink of coffee. There was no tremor in the hand that held the cup, no sign of alarm in the glance she cast at him from beneath her lashes.

'How long are you planning to keep me here?'

'I don't know. I mean, not for very long.'

'What's your name? You've lost your moustache, haven't you? And your sunglasses.'

'You can call me Jay,' he said thinly.

'But it isn't your real name? Okay, Jay, a polecat by any other name will smell as nasty. Say, look at these eggs! Did you cook them, Jay?'

He shook his head. She was too bright for words. But maybe she was putting on an act. Yes, that was it, he thought. She was scared out of her pants but she was determined not to betray the fact.

'If they don't please you I can have them cooked the way you prefer them.'

'Oh, don't bother. When you're hungry even this hog-food tastes good.'

'You've got decided views and opinions.'

'Just taste,' she said, starting in on the food. 'You're holding me for ransom, aren't you?'

'We're not holding you because we think your vital statistics are unique.'

'Knock that off,' she said warningly. 'If one of you characters as much as gives me a lewd look I'll maim you for life.'

'You're safe enough, Miss Regan. So long as you make things easy for us we'll make things easy for you.'

'You aren't the boss of the gang, Jay? That fat man is the boss, isn't he?'

'He's the boss.' Brad knew that he ought to leave, that he shouldn't be talking with her like this, but something compelled him to spin it out. He had never seen such a beautiful girl. He admired everything about her, especially her spirit.

'How much are you holding me for?' she demanded next.

'A million dollars.'

She shrugged, laid down her fork and took another swallow of coffee.

'Why not? In for a dime, in for a dollar. But you have given thought to the penalty you're laying yourself open for? I mean, what the police will do to you when they catch up with you won't be so nice.'

He laughed shortly.

'You should worry, Miss Regan. The

police won't catch us. We're too smart for the police.'

'You're too smart to believe what you're trying to make me believe, Jay. Don't tell me that you're not. You're kidding yourself, mister. You won't get away with it. People like you never do.'

She was attempting to rattle him, he realised, but she was trying it on with the wrong guy. All the same he hadn't expected the darker side of his thoughts to be reflected in this fashion.

He went to the door and gripped the handle.

'Wait, Jay.'

He waited, his eyes narrowing, an emotion striving inside him that made him angry.

'Don't get cute ideas about me, doll,' he said roughly. 'I've met your type before. Plenty. You can bluff the tail off a brass monkey. But not with me, sister, not with me.'

'You'll change your mind,' she said in a quiet voice. 'Listen,' she went on urgently, 'you're not like those other fellows. They dragged you into this, I bet, with a picture of riches and easy living for the rest of your natural. But it won't work out that way, Jay. I'm asking you to listen and I want you to listen carefuly. Are you willing to murder me, Jay, or even to stand back and see me murdered?'

For a moment Brad thought that the shock of her experience must have made her crazy. He laughed harshly.

'Murder? Who mentioned murder, for pete's sake?'

'It will come to it,' she said calmly. 'Consider. I know each and every one of you by sight. You don't have to be a genius to see how I can identify each and every one of you when the police catch you. And the police will catch you eventually, whether or not you collect the ransom money. If I'm alive I'll be in a position to put the finger on you; if I'm dead, then the chances of you all being identified are that much less. Do you think the fat man hasn't gone over the angles? Do you think he can afford to turn me loose on receipt of my father's ransom payment?'

She dropped her head and commenced sobbing. At that moment Brad was furious with himself and with her. He had an urge to go forward to her and comfort her. At the same time he wanted to slap her.

'You're crazy,' he heard himself snarling. 'You're not going to be hurt. Nobody is going to hurt you. Get it? I just wouldn't stand for it. Do you hear me, Miss Regan?'

She went on sobbing; her blonde hair had fallen over her face in a golden, shimmering veil. Her slim shoulders shook.

'Oh, hell,' Brad panted, in utter confusion.

Knuckles rapped the bedroom door.

'Are you there, Brad?'

'I'm here,' he answered Jack Royal.

He opened the door and went out to Royal, slamming it after him and thrusting home the bolts. Jack Royal eyed him in a puzzled fashion.

'What's up with her?' he growled.

'She's got this idea that we're going to kill her. Did you ever hear anything more stupid?'

'She's scared,' Royal said tonelessly. 'What do you expect? Don't worry. She'll simmer down. Look, those bolts will hold her. Come into the living-room, Brad. I've been mulling over what you said about hustling this up. Maybe we ought to hustle it up.'

'You're damn right we should,' Brad cried forcefully.

'Then let's discuss the lift,' Royal told him and led the way to the living-room.

CHAPTER SIX

Dick Knight – Otherwise Detective Sergeant Richard Knight, attached to the Kentburg Police Department – was a tall, leanly built man of thirty-five, with brown hair trimmed in a severe crew cut, grey alert eyes, and the kind of ruggedly handsome features usually associated with the heroes of all-action Western movies. He had begun his police career pounding a beat, but had rapidly improved his lot by dint of the use of his agile brain to the utmost of its capacity and the intelligent application of the fearless courage he was possessed with. Ambition, also, played a part in the story, of course, but Dick Knight's ambitions were not those overriding burnings that can make a man's name poison to his comrades and his enemies alike. Sensitive for a cop, he avoided the limelight, and would as soon let a brother officer take the credit he was rightly due as initiate a move which might subsequently land him, blushing, on a pedestal.

Dick Knight lived in a comfortable apartment on Court Boulevard, in the south side of the city and within easy driving distance of headquarters.

He had met Wesley Regan's daughter a year before, at a police ball, and fallen in love with her almost immediately he laid eyes on her, confounding the sceptics who sought foundation for their barren, materialistic idealogies.

True, at the time, Dick had no hint of the background that went with the beautiful blonde girl. They came together at the bar, had a few drinks, chatted, and then danced. It wasn't until next day that Dick discovered her relationship to the millionaire.

The news had hit him like a fist to the groin. Old Wes Regan's offspring? Well, well! What a pity. And how he had badgered her for a date on the following night!

She had agreed to his date, but, on reflection, Dick told himself the girl had simply found him amusing; moreover, she was away far out on the fringe of his private dreams, too far out ever to become anything more than a wishful thought in the context of cold and sober reckoning.

His over-sensitive nature dictated that the date be passed up, ignored. It was the first time he had played hookey thus with a dame.

Her phone call to his apartment on the next evening was a shock, but a most pleasant and stimulating shock.

'At least, you might have warned me that you couldn't keep our appointment,' she had said in a voice that vibrated with suppressed anger.

'Look, Miss Regan,' he had replied bluntly. 'I'm sorry. Believe me, I'm sorry. But I'm a guy who was taught to observe the realities of life and never to duck them. Last night at the ball you were beautiful Miss America to me. Today I learned you are actually Miss Billion Dollar Regan. Be reasonable. What do we have in common?'

That elicited a shattering lecture on his downright stupidity and his recognition of the validity of discrimination. Who was he to say who should be her friend? Was she not entitled to the freedom of selection he would dare to claim for himself?

'I'm sorry,' he had said weakly and contritely. 'Please forgive me Miss Regan.'

'I may or may not forgive you, Dick. The point is, do you wish to see me again?'

'Do I what!' he cried in rapture. 'When can I pick you up, and where?'

It was the beginning of their association. It was an unique association in a sense. Carol Regan went out of her way to prove that social intercourse, to be absolutely legitimate, must be conducted without reference to material wealth. Personality and integrity of character were the paramount factors.

They argued a lot on an intellectual level, on a social level. Carol lacked the basic animal warmth that Dick would have wished for, but she did have wit, intelligence and charm as well as beauty, and he hoped for the day when she would outgrow her emotional inhibitions and be the simple creature which she strove too mightily to portray.

She was a girl easily bored, and Dick had encouraged her to immerse herself in as many outside interests as she could cope with. For a month she had held down a job in a druggist's, making up some excuse to give to her father for her absence from home every day. That had come to an end on old Wes's finding out what his daughter was up to.

Her latest kick was this acting academy thing and the artists' colony at High Point. Dick didn't mind her practising to become an actress, even if she didn't have a hope of making the grade, but he wasn't so happy about her mixing with those long-haired pseudo dropouts. Still, he had to humour her and pretend that he understood and sympathised with her fads. Privately Dick believed that Carol's real cure would be found when she had married him and produce a clutch of kids.

Which took him to his relationship with Wesley Regan. Old Wes had frowned on his daughter's friendship with a common or garden cop from the very outset. He dreaded the dawning of the day when Carol would announce her intention of becoming the wife of Detective Sergeant Richard Knight. That might sound like a high-flown title when spoken slowly and in the proper cadence, but, fundamentally, it carried no more genuine weight than soda-jerk or even bar swamper.

Dick Knight didn't give a curse for Wesley Regan or his billions or trillions, or whatever amount of money he owned; he did care a lot for his daughter. He hoped that he might marry Carol eventually. But if old Wes cut Carol off without a penny it was just okay by him. As Carol herself had stated, a friendship like theirs should owe no allegiance to material wealth.

At present Dick was enjoying a few days from duty. On Wednesday Carol had fallen in with his suggestion that they go for a drive on Friday, setting out early to give them time to make a complete tour of the coastal beauty spots. Dick was mildly disappointed when his phone call to the mansion on Seaway Heights produced the news that Carol was still abed. He was slightly puzzled about the remark her father had made concerning her going off somewhere this morning. Of course Carol could have been referring to her proposed outing with him and had been reluctant to spell this out to Wes in so many words.

After making the call Dick tidied up his

apartment and went off to breakfast. He had intended breakfasting somewhere along the coast with the girl, but he was hungry, and if they would be making a late start he might as well fortify himself.

He returned to his apartment a scant thirty minutes later and dialled the Regan house once more. On this occasion it was Doris, the elderly housekeeper who answered him.

'Hi, Doris,' he greeted the woman cheerfully. He was on good terms with her, and, during the early days of his association with Carol, she had been of splendid assistance to them in the planning of their dates. 'Is Carol out of bed yet?' he added on the same bright note.

'What! Oh, yes... No, she isn't. That is– Oh, golly, Dick, he made me promise not to say anything to anyone. But I'm so worried. I don't like it at all. I can't understand why he doesn't want you to know...'

'Doesn't want me to know what?' Dick Knight burst out impatiently. 'Say, what's going on there, Doris? Is Carol ill?'

'I–I– Dick, hold on a minute till I make sure he's still outside.'

'Why can't I talk with Carol?' Dick demanded angrily.

'Give me a chance, will you? I'll tell you in a minute.'

'Okay, Doris. I'll wait.'

His brain became a battleground for

conflicting guesses and theories while he did wait. It seemed an age before the housekeeper resumed her link with him.

'It's this way, Dick... Oh, how can I explain when I don't know myself what is going on?'

'Listen, beautiful,' Dick said tersely, 'you communicate in ordinary, simple English. If you're absolutely inarticulate then give me the news in monosyllabic answers to my questions. Is Carol ill?'

'No. I– The truth is, Dick, that she isn't in the house at all. She went out last evening to that Art Academy. Sam drove her there in the limousine. Sam went to collect her again at ten. But she wasn't there.'

'She wasn't what?'

'You see, Dick. It's a mystery. It's why I can't explain it properly. She wasn't at the Academy when Sam called for her. It appears she left the place at nine o'clock. Sam told me this before Mr. Regan got to him. Now you'd think Travis had been struck dumb.'

'Doris, let's get this straight from the beginning. You're saying that Carol went to the Art Academy last night as usual, and that Travis went there at ten to collect her, only to discover she had left the Academy at nine o'clock.'

'That's exactly what happened, Dick.'

'And she hasn't been in touch with home

in any fashion since then?'

'It's the way it seems, Dick. When I asked Mr. Regan where she was, he said she was all right and not to mention her to anybody. Dick, do – do you think she has run off with somebody?'

She was voicing the idea that had just hit Dick Knight like a sickening body blow. It was a moment before he gathered his wits sufficiently to reply.

'Good lord, Doris, I don't know. We were to spend the day together. Look, is this absolutely all you can tell me?'

'I'm afraid so. I don't mind saying that I'm worried to death.'

'How do you judge Mr. Regan to be behaving?'

'Queer, to say the least. Very queer. I've never seen him so worried. He seems to be going about in a daze. I was passing his study a little while ago and he was talking on the phone to someone. He sounded terribly excited.'

'So he could have heard from Carol?'

'Yes, it's possible. But, Dick, whatever you do, don't let on that I told you this.'

'Don't worry,' Dick said blankly. 'Listen,' he added quickly, 'if anything turns up at your end– But, no, that's no good. I was going to ask you to keep calling, but you'd better not. I might not be here. I'll call you later, Doris.'

'Yes, all right, Dick. But if Mr. Regan's around it's going to be difficult to talk to you.'

'I understand. Then forget it. Don't worry. Just leave it to me.'

'Try and find out where she is, Dick.'

'Sure, sure...' He hung up. He fished a cigarette from his pocket and put it to his lips. He puffed at it absently without lighting it.

Carol had taken off with another guy.

Well, what else was he to believe in the circumstances? And when he got right down to thinking of it, hadn't he feared all along that she might resort to some weird trick to escape from the cotton wool-lined cage that old Wes kept her in? But why had she not taken him into her confidence? Was she, basically, nothing better than a neurotic scatterbrain that he would be well rid of?

He remained in his apartment until noon, hoping that Doris might call him with more information, even though he had decided she shouldn't bother. At lunch time he could stick it no longer. He felt that he must do something constructive if he wasn't to go crazy with worry.

His policeman's experience urged him that the best place to start was at the beginning. Carol definitely had gone to the Art Academy last night. Therefore the woman who managed the Academy should have noticed when she left. Perhaps the doorman could contribute something also.

He decided to commence by contacting the Academy.

A man came on in answer to his phone call. He was a carpenter, he explained, and there was no one on the premises but himself and his helper.

'Look,' Dick said, 'I know that a Miss Bridges runs the school. I wish to speak with her. I could look up her number, I suppose, but you might save me the trouble.'

'I have her number right enough,' the carpenter replied. 'I was at her house first thing this morning, getting her instructions. We're fixing the stage, you see, and–'

'What is her number, please?' Dick interrupted him.

The carpenter gave it to him, together with Miss Bridges' home address. Dick thanked him and broke the connection. He dialled Miss Bridges' home. A moment later he was talking with the woman.

'Hello, Miss Bridges. My name is Knight and I'm a close friend of Miss Carol Regan. Did you notice that she left your classes last night before her usual time?'

'Yes, she did, Mr. Knight. She went off without telling me she was going. But Jim Leasor – one of my male students – explained she had had a message from her father. Apparently her father was taken ill– By the way, Mr. Knight, Mr. Regan's condition is not too serious, I trust?'

'No, not really. I was speaking to him earlier and he seems in reasonable shape.'

'I'm so glad. Well, then ... was there something else you wished to ask me in connection with Miss Regan?'

Dick's thoughts were in a complete whirl. Somehow or other he contrived to answer clearly.

'No, thanks, Miss Bridges. But, yes–' He laughed shortly. 'I almost forgot what I meant to say in the first place. Carol imagines she mislaid her purse, and I wanted to ask the doorman at the Academy if he had spotted it.'

'Miss Regan lost her purse? How dreadful! Frank Burley is the doorman, but if Frank had noticed the purse he would have surrendered it to me at once.'

'Yes, I'm sure he would. It's just struck me that it might have slipped from his mind.'

'Oh!' The woman sounded a trifle stiff at that. 'Then I suggest that you call and see Frank, Mr. Knight. He resides at two, twenty-four, Bank Street.'

'Perhaps I won't bother after all. It was merely to prove to Carol that she must have lost it elsewhere.'

'I do understand, Mr. Knight. But you really should call on Frank in any case.'

'I guess I might, Miss Bridges. Forgive me for bothering you.'

'I assure you it was no bother, Mr. Knight. Goodbye.'

Dick said goodbye and hung up.

He stood for a long time staring at the telephone without seeing it. An alarm was beginning to stir at the back of his brain. Now he knew that Carol's reason for leaving the Academy at nine o'clock was that she had heard her father was ill. Jim Leasor had told Miss Bridges this. It meant he would have to see Jim Leasor. The name was vaguely familiar to him. Carol had mentioned it once or twice in connection with the acting school. She thought Leasor was a nice fellow. Sure he was nice! Perhaps he was so nice that Carol felt she just had to run away with him.

Dick stamped on this trend of thought straightaway. For one thing, he couldn't condemn Carol until he had the entire facts at his disposal; for another thing, he didn't really believe she had run away with anyone. There had to be a different answer.

The doorman might be able to shed some light.

Twenty minutes later Dick was parking his car at the kerb opposite an ancient brown and grey apartment building. After making sure he had the number right he went into the hall and checked the names on the mailboxes. Frank Burley was in 2D on the second floor.

Burley happened to be on his way out of the apartment as Dick walked along the dimly-lit passage. The man peered short-sightedly at him and said hallo.

'You looking for me?' he added.

'If you're Frank Burley, then I'd like a word with you, Frank.'

'Oh! Do you know, I had a feeling all morning I might be hearing from somebody.'

'What about?' Dick queried, following him back into the small living-room of the apartment. He took a chair and hooked his hat on the knob of his left knee.

'Let's wait until I learn what you're after,' the other responded with a dry chuckle.

'Miss Carol Regan?'

'You've hit it, mister. You've just hit it. Are you a cop? Nothing has happened to Miss Regan? It was a damned queer how-do-you-do to my way of thinking.'

'I'm a friend of Miss Regan,' Dick compromised. 'It appears that somebody played a trick on her last night. Maybe you could tell me a little more about it?'

'There isn't much I can tell. All the same it looked damned queer at the time. A trick, you say. Well, it was a dirty trick any way you view it.'

'What happened?' Dick urged brusquely.

Burley brought a cheap cigar from his vest pocket and searched for a match. Dick produced his lighter and flicked it for him.

'Thanks. Well, you see, I was at the door when this guy in uniform came into the entrance hall. I knew he was a chauffeur or something, on account of the uniform. But he wasn't the guy who usually calls for Miss Regan.'

'What did he say to you?'

'He just asked me to fetch Miss Regan quickly as her father had taken sick and wanted her immediately. What could I do but deliver his message to Miss Regan?'

'You delivered it to her in person?'

'No, I didn't. You see, Miss Bridges hates any kind of disturbance when she's taking a class. I stood at the door and signalled to Miss Regan that I wanted her. Young Mr. Leasor must have thought I was calling him. He came to the door and I asked him to give Miss Regan the message.'

'She left right away? Alone?'

'She left with the chauffeur. He was at the wheel of a big Caddy. Usually Travis waits until Miss Regan is seated before he gets into the car. I thought it odd. I opened the door for her, or at least I saw her into the car. It drove off. Then, at ten, Travis turns up for Miss Regan and I tell him what happened. He was in a Caddy too and he used the phone to call his boss. He got orders to go home, I guess, and that's all I can tell you.'

CHAPTER SEVEN

At this stage Burley became alarmed. Why was he being asked these questions? What had happened to Miss Regan? Had anything happened to her?

'It's okay, Frank. Cool off, will you?'

'Is the girl missing from home?' the doorman demanded bluntly. 'You cops beat around a thing without coming to the point.'

'I'm not a...' Dick started to say and let the rest of the sentence tail off. He began afresh. 'As I explained, Frank, I'm a friend of Miss Regan's. I was in touch with the lady who runs the academy. Miss Regan mislaid her purse last night. She asked me to try and find it, and—'

'Is that all?' Burley said with a high laugh. 'The way you were talking, I thought something was wrong with Miss Regan. No, I didn't see her purse. If I'd seen her purse I would have handed it to Miss Bridges.'

'Don't worry about it, Frank.' Dick was anxious to get away from the man now. Burley was anything but the slow thinker he appeared to be at a glance. There was the chance of him making this call the subject for gossip later. 'I hope you will just forget that I ever visited.'

'Well, I don't know. Miss Bridges is bound to ask me about the purse too.'

Dick Knight had an instinct about the way the wind was shifting direction. He rarely handed out money, either to elicit information or to suppress loose talk, but this was one occasion when he felt justified in plucking a five-spot from his billfold and waving it beneath a man's nose.

Burley accepted it.

'You can't kid me you're not a cop,' he said. 'But I'm smart enough to keep my nose clean.'

'And your mouth buttoned,' Dick said quietly, patting him on the shoulder and leaving him.

On the street he sat in his car and smoked a cigarette. His forehead was grooved in lines of worried thought and his eyes were screwed up narrowly in concentration.

The picture was now thus: Carol had gone to the Art Academy last night as was her custom. She should have remained at the place until ten o'clock, when Sam Travis, the Regan chauffeur would call to take her home. Instead another chauffeur, driving a Cadillac, had turned up at the Academy at nine o'clock. He had spun a story about Wes Regan being ill, and Carol had gone off with him. She had not been seen at home since.

Who was the other chauffeur and where

had he taken Carol?

Had Carol deliberately set up the act for reasons of her own, intending to go off with somebody and wanting to cast a smoke screen of confusion for the benefit of him and her father?

If Carol had really done this, she wasn't worth bothering about. On the other hand, if someone had wanted to snatch her, then the entire business reeked of an elaborate and well-organised kidnap plot.

Dick's blood ran cold at the thought.

He smoked half of the cigarette and tossed the butt through the window. The Cadillac, he thought, there might be a clue there. If a kidnap plot had been arranged, the kidnappers would have mapped out a chart of the girl's movements. They would have discovered how she was driven to the Art Academy, left there, and was picked up again at ten o'clock. What better way to snatch her than to have a matching Cadillac call at nine, with the bombshell that her father was ill and wanted her immediately?

Cold sweat plastered the detective's brow as he considered this seriously.

He drove on along the street until he reached a pay phone, then, shut in the booth, he put a ring in to Police Headquarters. Don Berman was at the desk and gave him a cheerful greeting.

'What's the matter, Dick?' he asked. 'Can

you not find anything to do with your spare time?'

'Listen, Don, this is strictly confidential. Do you have a report of a missing car? It might have been stolen yesterday or a few days ago?'

'That's a damn silly question, Dick. You know we average at least three stolen cars per day. What make of heap is it you've found?'

'I haven't found it. It's simply a notion I have. This would be a maroon Cadillac Fleetwood Sedan. A two-year old, I think.'

'You aren't kidding me, Dick? You aren't drunk?'

'I'm not kidding and I'm not drunk. Have a look-see, Don, like a good guy.'

'Give me a minute.'

Dick trapped a fresh cigarette in his lips while he waited for Berman to come through.

'Yeah, Dick, you might have got something there. A heap answering your description was stolen from outside the Grinwald Theatre on Wednesday night. It belongs to an Arnold Huntmeyer. But wait for the punch line. Huntmeyer has got his car back again.'

'When did he get it back?'

'Patrolman Binkley came on it early this morning on Natchez Avenue.'

'And Huntmeyer has recovered it?' Dick groaned.

'I told you so, didn't I?'

'Listen, Don, do me a favour. See if you can wangle for a guy from the fingerprint section to visit Huntmeyer. He can tell Huntmeyer we've got a line on the car thief. Have the fingerprint guy give the car the complete works and make a record of every print he finds inside and out.'

'Well, all right, Dick. But look, why don't you call round and tell us what you're on to?'

'It's merely a hunch I've got. Be in touch with you later, Don. Oh, make sure Huntmeyer's prints are taken for the purpose of eliminating him.'

'Would you believe it? The idea would never have occurred to me.'

'See you, pal.'

Dick hung up and left the booth. In his car once more he went into another deep huddle. A Cadillac had been stolen on Wednesday night and had been found early this morning. The kidnappers could have borrowed the car, used it for their trick, and then ditched it. But if these kidnappers actually existed, where had they taken Carol?

The detective reflected on his chat with Doris Maddox, the Regan housekeeper. Why had Wes Regan told him that his daughter was in bed when in fact she had been missing since last night? The answer was simple and shattering. The kidnappers had been in touch with Wesley. They had already commenced putting the squeeze on him. The squeeze would be for nothing else but loot, lots of loot. They were taking a gigantic risk and the reward would have to be commensurate with the risk. Had they given Regan instructions?

If only Regan would take him into his confidence.

If only he could talk with Travis, the chauffeur, and hear what he had to say.

Regan would have zipped Travis up, and plenty. It was a miracle that Doris had seen fit to tell him what she knew. Bless you, Doris, he thought. You may have provided me with the lead that could save her.

As Dick saw the problem, his next move was too obvious to be missed. He had to talk with Wesley Regan, and the hell with the consequences.

An old lady was using the phone booth and Dick waited impatiently until she emerged. Then he went in and dialed the millionaire's number. There was a response to his call almost at once.

'Yes?' Wesley Regan said in an eager bark. 'Mr. Regan here.'

'Hello, Mr. Regan. This is Dick Knight again. I–'

'You're too late, Dick,' the other cut in on him. 'Carol has just left ten minutes ago.'

'I see,' Dick murmured. 'But you did tell her that I rang?'

'Of course I did,' Regan snapped. 'She said something about getting in touch with you later.'

'Did she leave by herself?'

'That's right. No, she didn't! You know I don't want her at the wheel of a car. She left with her friend she's spending the day with.'

'A girl?'

'Look, Dick, what is this – a third-degree or something? Carol must be free to choose her own friends, but if it will set your mind at rest, the friend who collected Carol was a girl.'

Dick paused for a moment before speaking.

'Mr. Regan,' he said firmly. 'I want to talk with you. I'm driving out there now and I hope you will see me.'

'Talk with me!' The millionaire gave a shrill whinny of a laugh. 'I'm afraid it won't be this morning, Dick. I'm kind of busy right now, and–'

'I don't care how busy you are,' Dick said sharply, reverting to his businesslike cop manner. 'I'm coming out to see you, and I want you to be there when I arrive.'

He didn't wait for a reply, but slammed the receiver down on its rest and left the booth. He got into his car and set off through the streets to gain the suburbs and Seaway Heights.

His determination was no less solid by the

time he came off the curving coast road and followed the winding driveway through the flat, dry heat of the morning to the huge sprawling house that had a line of razor-back hills for a backcloth and the blue, hazy, rumbustious Pacific not more than fifty feet from the front yard.

Even so, Dick knew the little needling of uneasiness that always accompanied his visits to this house of wealth. He guessed it was a throwback to the days – not so far removed – when his antecedents had shuffled up to rear porches, battered hats in hands, begging for charity.

There was a stiff thrust to his shoulders and an exaggerated swagger to his gait as he mounted the steps and pushed his thumb into the bell button. He heard the muted thrum of a motor mower and caught the peculiar scent of grass cuttings. His nostrils reacted.

A Filipino houseboy opened the door and flashed his teeth at Dick. He said in a friendly way, 'Hi, Sergeant Knight.'

'Hi yourself, Sunshine.' Dick would have buttonholed the servant had Wesley Regan not appeared at that moment in the hall behind him.

'This is somewhat irregular, Dick. I told you I was tied up, and I meant precisely what I said.'

'I'm sorry,' Dick said in a neutral voice.

Regan made a meagre gesture with his arm and the houseboy stood aside to allow the detective to enter. The millionaire took him to his study and made a curt motion towards a chair opposite his desk. Dick sat down and hooked his hat on the knob of his left knee. He met the hard eyes that wrestled with his own before sliding slowly to a carved bronze paper weight on the polished desk top.

'Would you care for a drink, Dick?'

'No, thank you, sir. It's a bit early in the day for me. Have one for yourself by all means.'

'I don't drink this early, myself,' Regan said in an abstracted fashion. 'Cigar?' He pushed the box forward.

'I'll smoke a cigarette if you don't mind.'

Dick lit his cigarette, assimilating all the impressions he had gained so far. In no degree did they alleviate the cold, sickening dismay that weighed on him.

'All right, you wanted to see me. What do you want to see me about?'

'Carol.'

For an instant it seemed that Wes Regan had been turned into stone. His facial muscles froze, as did the animation in his eyes. For all Dick knew the millionaire might have ceased breathing at the same time.

Then, 'Carol?' in a hoarse whisper followed by that ridiculous whinny of a laugh.

'You've gotten round to asking her to marry you, Dick–'

'I haven't gotten round to asking her to marry me. But I hope to do so at some date in the future.'

'Oh!' The hard eyes fused with the detective's gaze, oscillated briefly before steadying and narrowing. 'What else could you have to talk about?'

Dick leaned forward in his chair.

'I'm not going to pull any punches with you, Mr. Regan. I'd be failing in my duty to my conscience and to your daughter if I did so. I'm going to give it to you straight from the shoulder, and when I do, you can tell me to get the hell to minding my own business if you feel like it. I trust you won't do that. I trust you will realise that my interference is calculated to produce the proper results.'

'Interference? Proper results? What in blue blazes are you trying to put over on me, Dick?'

'I'm not trying to put anything over on you. I'm saying that I want you to be totally honest with me. Where is Carol?'

Regan rocked back in his chair as though he'd been shot. Had Dick required conclusive evidence that Carol Regan really was in trouble, then this was it.

'Where is Carol?' the millionaire echoed at length. 'Didn't I tell you where she is? She's spending the day with a friend.'

'What is the name of the friend.'

'How the hell do I know what her name is?' Regan erupted. 'Now, see here, Dick, I'm willing to overlook a lot from you, seeing as how you're a cop, but if you figure you have the right to subject me to an inquisition, then your figuring's all wrong. Get it?'

Regan stood up, neck red and bulging, the muscles of his jaws dancing in an agitated spasm. He made a violent sweeping motion with a thick-fingered hand.

'Sit down, Mr. Regan.'

'I'll be damned if I sit down,' Regan roared.

'Okay,' Dick snapped. 'Please yourself. But you're not chasing me before I'm ready to leave. You're not intimidating me either. I'm interested in the whereabouts of Carol, and I'm not leaving this house until you make an honest attempt to satisfy my curiosity.'

'Honest!' Wesley Regan sneered. 'Curiosity! What do you think you are? Who do you think you're talking to? Goddamn you, Dick, you will leave my house, even if I have to have you thrown out.'

'Sit down, Mr. Regan.'

'Go stuff yourself,' Regan raged. He did sit down finally. He snatched a cigar from the box at his hand, began to unwrap it, and then, in a fit of frustration, crumpled the tobacco to shreds between his fingers and flung the resultant mess to the floor. He glared at the detective with unadulterated malevolence.

'Okay,' he said quaveringly. 'You think you're smart. You think that Carol and I had a row and she has taken off to cool down. Is that what you believe?'

Perhaps it was what he wanted Dick to believe. In his desperation Wesley Regan was bringing all his resources of cunning to bear. Was this really what had happened? No, the detective thought fleetingly, he was being given a sniff of a red herring.

'Let me put this to you,' he began quietly. 'I know that Carol went to her acting lesson at the Art Academy as usual last night. I also know that she left at nine o'clock and not at her customary time of ten o'clock. She was driven off in a Cadillac. The Cadillac had been stolen on the previous night. The car was left abandoned down in town. The police have recovered this car and returned it to its owner. You say that Carol came home here last night, that she went to bed in this house, that she rose this morning and went out with a girl friend–'

'Who have you been talking to?'

'Right now I'm talking to you, Mr. Regan. Let me put something else to you. It is a theory that I have formed. Carol was drawn from her acting class last night by a trick.

She got into a Cadillac which she imagined was being driven by Sam Travis. As far as I'm concerned, and as far as you're concerned, Carol vanished into thin air after that. I believe she's been kidnapped.'

'Kidnapped? You're crazy! You're completely out of your mind, Knight. Have you turned in this crazy story to the department?'

'This is something else which I want to impress on you, sir. I have not turned in any story. I'm supposed to be taking a break from my duties. I wouldn't have been so curious if Carol and I had not arranged to spend the day together. The result is that I've come up against a bunch of hard facts that I refuse to turn a blind eye on. Now, if Carol has been kidnapped I want you to tell me so. If the kidnappers have made contact with you I want you to tell me so. Then we'll be able to meet the problem as it ought to be met and as it must be met. You don't have to worry about me spilling the beans. Carol means as much to me as she does to you, and I wouldn't make a solitary move that could put her in danger. Do you understand what I'm saying?'

Wesley Regan was silent for several dragging seconds, and, studying him, Dick could divine the veritable hell he was going through. Should he trust him or shouldn't he? Would it be wise to take a cop into your confidence and place your daughter's life and future in his hands?

Just when it seemed that Regan would fall into pieces and blubber out the whole woeful story, he pulled himself together. He filled his lungs with air and laid his hard eyes unblinkingly on the young man before him.

'You're nuts, Dick,' he said scornfully. 'And if you've got an ounce of sense left in your head you'll forget this whole silly scene. Why, man, if I believed there was the slimmest possibility of—'

'That is your last words?' Dick interrupted bleakly.

'I'd say, for your sake, that it better be,' was the ominous rejoinder.

Dick sighed and came to his feet, clamping his hat on his head. 'I'm sorry you don't trust me, sir. I wish you did. But whatever happens I'll do nothing that could bring risk to Carol.'

He left the study, went along the hall to reach the door. Outside he hesitated momentarily, then, realising there was nothing further to be accomplished here for the present, he headed on to his car.

CHAPTER EIGHT

Jack Royal's plan for collecting the ransom money was simple and clear-cut. He had considered a dozen elaborate ideas, he explained to Brad, but discarded them all eventually in favour of a straightforward pick up and walk away, as he termed it.

'You can work out a hundred permutations on a few ideas, but when you get right down to ground level the basic fact remains. Somebody is going to carry a million bucks to us and somebody is going to have to carry it away.

'The biggest difficulty, as I saw it, was finding a stretch of road to suit the purpose. The pick-up point cannot be too close to town and yet not too far away from it. If we decided to do this in the country we would be putting ourselves at a disadvantage. There are side roads, fields, undergrowth, where a guy could lie in hiding and watch what was going on.'

'That wouldn't do him much good unless he could definitely put the finger on us afterwards,' Brad said. 'Are you thinking of a cop or cops?'

'A guy could lie somewhere and use a

movie camera,' Royal said, his narrow mouth puckering tightly at the corners. 'I've always had this notion about a movie camera. The uses it can be put to, I mean.'

'I follow you, Jack. Maybe deep down inside of you lurks a frustrated movie maker.'

Royal didn't think the joke was funny. He had made his preamble, and if it fell on deaf ears, then that was that. So long as Brad was able to concentrate on the essentials he didn't have to worry.

He produced a sheet of paper that had a crude map drawn on it and spread it on the table in front of Brad. He traced with a blunt fingertip and kept talking.

'This heavy line here is the main road leading from Kentburg to Dorton. About ten miles out on the Dorton road there is a stretch that runs parallel with the ocean. I've scouted it thoroughly and I know what I'm talking about. On the ocean side there isn't enough room for a fly to hide never mind a cop, if Regan's nerve should break at the last moment and he calls for the cops. On the east side of the road – here,' Royal shifted his fingernail to a dark smudge, 'there is an elevated second-class road that used to be the main link with Dorton before they laid the new highway. Here too is a thick stand of trees that will make an ideal shield and vantage point. It looks directly down on the main road. Now, a quarter mile further to the north there is a fork where the old road meets the highway and where another minor road doubles back towards Kentburg–'

'I know where it is,' Brad interrupted him. 'I know the exact spot you're talking about. So you're going to have Regan drive out of town in a car, bringing the loot with him, stop a quarter mile short of the fork, at a spot where we can observe him without being seen.'

'You've got it so far, Brad.'

'Just a minute, Jack. You intend Regan to make the drive by himself. Does he drive himself?'

'Of course he does.'

'There's absolutely no doubt of it, I hope?'

'I'm telling you, Brad.'

'Okay. Regan drives there on his own, stops a quarter mile short of the fork as per instructions. What does he do then?'

'He'll leave the car,' Royal explained. 'He'll start walking back into the direction he came from.'

'There could be a snag there. The old guy might not be too brisk on his feet. A patrol vehicle could cruise up and ask him what's the matter.'

'I've thought of this. For a start, Wes Regan is as nimble on his feet as a mountain goat. If he should be stopped before we can

110

make the lift he'll say that his car gave out on him and he's walking to find help.'

Brad thought it over for a little. He didn't expect for a moment that the trick would go off like a dream, although he had every hope that it would.

'All right. Let's say he leaves the car and takes off on foot. There is the car sitting with the million bucks aboard – we trust – and it looks as though it is empty. What if it isn't empty? What if there is a cop ducking low with a gun, ready to open up at the first guy who approaches?'

Jack Royal frowned slightly.

'If you were in Wes Regan's shoes and you loved your daughter the way he does, would you risk her life by playing a prank on her kidnappers?'

'No, I guess I wouldn't.'

'Neither will Regan. Look, Brad, there's bound to be the element of danger, but I've got it whittled down so small that it's practically non-existent.'

'It's non-existent so long as Regan plays ball. We're depending on Regan doing so. Okay, you'll let him walk along the road a little. If a patrol car stops he'll say his car has given up. The cops will see what they can do to help. We'll see them, naturally, and make ourselves scarce. But what happens if they get suspicious when the car starts and they decide to search it?'

'Oh, be your age, Brad. Wes Regan is Wes Regan. Everybody knows him. If the car starts under the magic of the cops they'll let it go at that.'

'Okay,' Brad said again. 'He walks off and we give him time to get clear. Then we get to the car, grab the dough and hotfoot it. How is this to be arranged?'

'Pete will be waiting at the fork in a car. He'll be able to keep tabs on events with binoculars. I've got a swell set of night glasses for the job. Pete will watch Regan leave the car. He'll stay where he is until he sees the lift being made, then he'll drive out fast, help to dump in the suitcases, turn around and drive back to the fork. From there he'll keep going towards Kentburg, go on to the Bridgeport road and finish up here in the hills.'

'This means you'll have a car on the elevated road as well, and take off immediately the trick is accomplished?'

'That's right,' Royal agreed.

'You've already gone over this with Pete?'

'Of course. It's so simple a kid could do it blindfold. But even so, we can't afford to make the slightest mistake.'

'So Pete will be at the fork in a car. Pete will be on his own until he lifts the suitcases and the guy who fetches them from Regan's car?'

Royal nodded.

'I'll be above in my own car. At the outset you will be with me.'

'Who is going to take the suitcases from Regan's wagon?'

'You are, Brad.'

Brad stared at him.

'Roy? Where does he fit in? You're leaving him to mind the girl?' Brad didn't like that at all.

'That's right. You're the most active of the four of us. You've got a cool nerve. You'll do it Brad.' It was an order that invited no argument.

'What will you be doing, Jack?'

'I'll be watching the whole operation. I'll have glasses too so that I can follow the progress of Regan while he's walking. At the right moment I'll give you the signal. I've studied the track leading from the high road to the main one. The descent might be pretty rough, Brad, but it shouldn't give you much trouble going down there.'

Perhaps not, Brad thought fleetingly. He was active and sure-footed. He failed to see how clambering down the slope would bother him. All the same, he would be the guy in the open when the ball commenced. He would be out there, on foot, defenceless except for the gun he would carry. A gun wouldn't see him through if Wesley Regan made a pact with the cops and the whole countryside became flooded with them.

Pete Kripp would be in his car, ready to take off at the slightest sign of danger. Royal would be up on the side road with his car, and Roy Judge would be high and dry at the cabin.

'Are you scared, Brad?'

It wasn't a gibe or a taunt; it was a plain, straightforward question. Brad accepted it as such.

'Just a little,' he admitted with a faint grin.

'You wouldn't be human if you weren't,' Royal said with a shrug of his heavy shoulders. 'But it ought to go off without a hitch.'

'One more point, Jack. There is the danger that Regan will make a deal with the cops at the moment of truth. I'm down there on the road and suddenly the place is alive with them. What happens in that event?'

'You'll have a choice,' Royal said as though he had been waiting for the question. 'If the worst comes to the worst Pete will send his car to you immediately. You can either take advantage of this or climb into Regan's car and make your own break. The prevailing circumstances will give you the lead on your best bet. If you do use Regan's car – and there aren't cops stashed there as well – then you'll be on your own for a while. If you jump in with Pete he'll decide which is the best direction to take. But I really can't see the old guy pulling a fast one on us.'

Brad was silent for a while as he considered every aspect of the proposed manoeuvre. It hadn't required a genius to dream it up and it wouldn't need a genius to put it into operation, but it would require the application of a certain amount of courage and cold nerve.

'It looks all right to me, Jack,' he said finally.

'Then you're on, Brad?'

'Could I get out of it now if I wanted out?'

'You'd be a stupe to turn your back on the chance of a lifetime. You don't really want out?'

'No I don't want out. But there is just one more bug that I'd like to dispose of.'

'You name it, I try to fill the bill,' Royal said, in an expansive mood now.

'The girl,' Brad began, holding the squat man's eyes with his own. 'Something might go wrong. No matter how carefully you plan there can be a hitch. So okay. If there's a hitch and we miss out on a million peanuts, what about the girl?'

'What about her?' Royal asked roughly. 'She's fine and healthy, isn't she?'

'Yes, she is. And here's my sole sucker punch, Jack. She must remain in that condition.'

Royal laughed harshly.

'You damn fool, Brad! Do you figure I might eat her for breakfast? I've got a sister, remember?'

'I've got your word for it, Jack?'

'Of course you have. Now, see here, friend, I might be a tough old cookie and I mightn't care much where I plant my big feet when I'm in a hurry to some place, but under here–' he thumped his chest and showed Brad a view of his teeth '–there is nothing but twenty-one carat gold.'

'Then it's settled,' Brad said slowly. 'You were going to put it off a few days to let Wes Regan stew. You said you would hustle it up. How much are you hustling?'

'We'll make it on Sunday night. I'd go into action tomorrow night, but that would be rushing it too fast, Brad. Sunday night that road will be quiet and will suit our plan.'

Brad would have preferred getting it over and done with on Saturday night. As he had explained to Royal before, the longer they held on to the girl the greater grew the risk of Wesley Regan breaking under the strain and going to the police. But the squat man needed the time to organise the preliminaries, he supposed, and he would gain nothing by attempting to pressure him.

Roy Judge got back to the house a half hour later. Pete Kripp turned in to catch up on some sleep and Royal told Brad to stand guard at the girl's bedroom door.

'I wanted to go for a walk in the fresh air,' Brad complained. 'The dame would need to be a Houdini to get past those bolts on the door.'

'What's so tiresome about making like a watchdog for the pretty lady?' Judge queried with his neighing laugh. 'I bet if you were on the other side of the door you wouldn't even think of walking in the woods.'

'That isn't funny, Roy,' Brad retorted thinly. 'You're not having fancy ideas?'

'Who, me? Pull yourself into a single life-like piece, man. I wouldn't touch a snooty bitch like that with a ten-foot pole.'

'You guys knock it off,' Jack Royal grunted sourly. 'Brad, I want you to stay guard by the door.'

'All right, Jack. I'm on my way.'

He sat on the stool by the door and smoked cigarettes. He was sitting there for twenty minutes when there was a soft tap on the inside of the panel.

'What is it, Miss Regan?'

'Does the fat man object to my having a cigarette?'

It could be a trick, Brad reflected, ever ready to suspect her of a trick. She had turned out to be anything but a drooping lily and he was prepared to grant her all the spunk a woman could be capable of.

'Why do you want a cigarette? Are you planning to set fire to your room?'

'You've given me an idea, Jay. I got a whiff of your tobacco smoke despite those bolts on the door.'

Brad said nothing in reply. He canted his head hopefully, waiting for her to resume the conservation. All was silent in the bedroom.

He rose and slid the bolts back carefully. Just as carefully he pushed the door inwards. It came up against the inner lock.

'What do you want?' she said in a frightened whisper.

'To offer you a cigarette.'

'Are you alone out there?'

His pulse began hammering for some reason. It showed you what an honourable guy you would be if temptation only polished up its horns, he thought bitterly.

'Yeah,' he said shortly.

The lock snicked off and the door opened fractionally. The hazel eyes fused with his own and then lowered and were hooded.

'Here is a cigarette.' His voice was thick and he cursed himself for a silly punk.

She took the cigarette and placed it between her lips. She did so, unconscious of the effect the simple action had on him. He flicked his lighter and his fingers trembled badly.

'Thanks, Jay.' She puffed and stood back from him. He made no effort to pull the door to.

'Are you feeling okay?'

'I'm as well as I can be,' she said, looking

directly at him again.

'Don't worry,' he said. 'Everything is going to turn out fine.'

'If you say it to yourself often enough you're bound to believe it in the end.'

'You're just trying to rattle me, aren't you?'

'Why should I rattle you? You strike me like a fellow who could get nasty if you took it into your head.'

'I never get nasty with women.'

'Never? You're pulling my leg, naturally. But you aren't out of the same mould as those other three.'

'They broke the mould when they saw how my halo might start a fashion.'

Brad went to close the door. The girl moved nearer and gripped the edge of it.

'Wait,' she said in a low-pitched tone. 'Listen...'

'Sorry,' he said gruffly. 'Jack would have my hide if he found me fraternising.'

'You're frightened of him?'

'Plenty.'

'So am I,' she said tautly, her gaze digging into his own. 'I don't trust him. I wouldn't trust him an inch. He's the sort of man would leave his best friend in the lurch.'

'Spare me the dramatics, baby.'

'I'm trying to make you see sense, Jay. You're not in the same league as those fellows. You've got feelings, a conscience about

119

this. I can read it in your face, your eyes. You might have a girl-friend. If you have, can you imagine her in a situation similar to this? Would you sleep easy at night, knowing that her life hung in the balance, that she could be molested, raped, and not a person there to lift a hand to save her?'

'Enough of that talk,' he snarled. 'I gave you my word, didn't I? I said nobody was going to touch you and I meant exactly what I said.'

'So you've got your Superman outfit in your hip pocket, ready to put it on when the going becomes really tough?'

'Lay off, Miss Regan. Do you want another cigarette to light from that one?'

She nodded and accepted the second cigarette. Her fingers curled about his hand and the long nails dug in sharply.

'How much are they paying you for your share, Jay?' she said throatily. 'A quarter of the take? Two hundred and fifty thousand dollars? Well, you listen to me and listen good. Get me out of this mess and I'll see to it that you get a half million dollars. No strings attached whatever.'

A wave of anger burst through him and he slammed the door in her face, thrusting home the bolts violently.

The little conniving tramp, he thought. The goddamn little conniving tramp. What did she take him for – some kind of half-baked nut? Well, he would just show her. The hell if he wouldn't show her.

He wished with every fibre of his being that it was Sunday and they were going into action and that he would never lay eyes on that dame again in his life.

CHAPTER NINE

Dick Knight waited until two o'clock before calling headquarters again. Don Berman was still holding down the desk and greeted him with a trace of excitement in his voice.

'Hey, Sherlock, a fingerprint man subjected that car of Huntmeyer's to the full works. The only prints he could find belonged to Huntmeyer himself.'

'Is that so?' Dick knew a sharp stab of disappointment. If prints had been found in the car they could have been checked against the records of local crooks. He knew at least a score of would-be bigshots around town, and he was pretty certain that the kidnap effort on Carol – for by this time he was firmly convinced that Carol Regan was a kidnap victim – had been carried out by locals with the opportunity of studying her background and keeping close track of her movements.

'You don't sound so happy about it, Dick. What did you hope to uncover?'

'Not a lot,' he replied to the desk sergeant. 'I merely had a hunch.'

'It might be a good one, pal. Ordinary punks stealing a car and driving around for kicks don't usually go to the trouble of removing all their fingerprints.'

'The thief could have been wearing gloves,' Dick said vaguely and hung up.

He hoped he hadn't seemed too abrupt to Don. Berman had expected him to open up on his hunch and he hadn't done so. Perhaps he should turn his findings over to headquarters and recruit all the aid that was available.

No, it was too early to call on the big guns. Once he mentioned the word kidnap it would open a floodgate he would be unable to control. He must consider Wesley Regan and his anxiety for his daughter's safety and welfare. He must take every angle into consideration before making a rash move. What he required most at the moment was information relating to likely suspects.

Dick spent the afternoon going through the bars and joints where information might be tapped from characters who talked at a price. He drew nothing but blank after blank, due mainly, he supposed, to the fact that he couldn't mention any specific line of inquiry he was following.

It was dusk and he was feeling weary and defeated when he wandered into a pool hall on Denver Avenue. Not all of the habitués knew him by sight, although most of them could smell a cop at a hundred yards distance. They gave the detective a wide berth, and a couple of specimens remembered suddenly that they had urgent business to attend to elsewhere.

Dick hung around for a while, smoking and pretending a casual interest in the games going on at the tables. He was on the point of leaving when a skinny, gaunt-faced man sidled up to him and laid lean, claw-like fingers on his arm.

'Well, well, if it ain't Mr. Knight.'

Dick turned his head to glance at him. He took interest when he recognised Anse Weaver. Once upon a time Anse Weaver had been one of the best safe-crackers in the country, but age had blunted his touch and his enthusiasm, and, when he was put away for three short terms on the trot, the safe-cracker had seen the light and decided that the good, easy life was permanently beyond his reach.

'Hello, Anse,' Dick said with a wry grin. 'How goes it these days?'

'Not too well, Mr. Knight, not too well. Say, what brings you to this side of the tracks? Are we breeding them with guts in this quarter for a change?'

'You might know, Anse. I wouldn't. Well, it was nice seeing you old-timer. I've got to be going.'

Dick was half-way to the door when Weaver shuffled after him and laid his claws on his arm once more.

'Look, Mr. Knight, maybe if you told me what kind of rock you want to turn over I might be able to do you a favour.'

The old guy was evidently desperate for a hand-out and Dick peeled five dollars from his billfold and slipped them to him.

'Go somewhere and get yourself a square meal, dad.'

He went on out of the hall and stood on the sidewalk, peering up and down the neon-lit canyon. He was surprised to discover Anse Weaver still at his heels.

'Has that fellow Gilbert been hijacking trucks again?' he said with a mirthless cackle.

'Gilbert?' Dick said and frowned as he delved into his memory. He failed to couple the name with anything significant.

'Yeah, you know him. He hangs about here a lot. Likes to play pool. Likes to drink whisky and water over there in Gilly's Bar. Haven't seen him in the avenue for a couple of days, though.'

'Oh, I have you now, Anse. He was a trucker, wasn't he? His truck was taken from him one night.' It was all coming back to the detective.

'That's him. Hardly ever misses a night playing pool. Last time I saw him was on Tuesday. He was at one of the tables when that guy Judge came in and took him away–'

'Judge? You're talking of Roy Judge, Anse?' Dick knew Judge to be a man who had come under police suspicion on various occasions in connection with store robberies, auto-thefts and minor protection rackets. Auto-theft! But no, it was too much of a long shot.

'That's the guy,' Weaver's voice cut across the detective's thoughts. 'Not that I've got a lot against Brad Gilbert, though. He's not a bad sport. But I don't have to tell you what Roy Judge is.'

'So Judge came into the pool hall and took Gilbert away?' Dick murmured with apparent disinterest. 'Where did they go?'

'Don't ask me. If you could tell me what you're driving at, I could maybe trail my ear to the ground for a day or so.'

'I'm not driving at anything in particular, Anse.'

'Okay, okay. I just figured I could help you. Maybe another truck-load of cigarettes has grown wings?'

'There was no question of Gilbert being charged with being implicated,' Dick reminded the character.

'Don't tell me. I can read, can't I? I can cotton to a rumour as well as the next guy. Anyhow, Judge talked with Brad and Brad didn't go for him much. Then Brad looked like he might be scared of something and they went out together.'

'But you don't know where?'

'I said so, didn't I? But they did go as far

as Gilly's together.'

Dick stared through the neon-shot shadows at the gaunt features and a wan grin strove to his face.

'Sorry, Anse, you're barking up the wrong tree. I've got no more dough to spare. I'm not interested in Gilbert or Judge in any case.'

'Hey, hold on, Mr. Knight, I'm not a vampire. Do me a favour, will you?'

He shambed off into the gloom and Dick watched his progress over the road to Gilly's Bar. The faint smile of amusement melted from his mouth and eyes.

Was it such a long shot, he wondered again. But of course it was. It didn't warrant a second thought. As far as the department was concerned, the ex-truckie called Brad Gilbert didn't even rate a blob on a clean sheet of paper. But Roy Judge... Yes, there was a different kettle of fish. Perhaps it would not be amiss to hunt up Judge and have a confab. Why start with Judge, though? If there was skulduggery in the making, Gilbert would be the weakest link in the chain, due to his comparative innocence of crime. Therefore Gilbert was the person to see first of all.

Dick wished he could rid himself of the sensation of clutching at fragile straws. If he chose to be honest with himself he would realise that he was groping in the dark, without the slimmest hope of one solid clue to the disappearance of Carol Regan emerging.

'But if I don't do something constructive I'll go nuts,' he muttered savagely.

It was ten minutes before Anse Weaver emerged from Gilly's, and when he did Dick was waiting in the shadows for him.

'Hold a minute, Anse.'

'Now take it easy, Mr. Knight,' Weaver said with some alarm. He had taken on a load in a very short time with the result that his mood was verging on the cantankerous.

'I'm not going to bite you, old-timer. You've made me curious. Where does this bird Gilbert go to roost?'

'Oh, is that all? He lives out on the edge of town somewhere. Calbrook Street, I think.'

'You mean Holbrook, don't you?'

'Yeah, that's it. Look, Mr. Knight, I got to see a man about a dog...'

'Sure, Anse. Keep going, dad. Hold on to something for tomorrow.'

Dick left him and walked a block to where he had parked his car. It was a fine evening, with the sky on fire with billions of cold, glittering stars. It took him thirty minutes fighting through the traffic to gain the suburbs where Holbrook Street was located. It was a quarter crowded with cheap apartment buildings that outnumbered the private residences Dick guessed Gilbert would have lodgings in one of the apartment houses and picked on one at random. There was no Gilbert named on any of the mailboxes in the hall and he went on to rap at the manager's door.

The manager was an elderly, bald man and said he was sorry he couldn't assist him in tying down anyone called Gilbert.

'I suggest you just keep looking until you see his name listed, if he's living on this street.'

'What a good idea.'

Dick thanked him and left. He tried the hallways of four more similar buildings without better luck, but struck oil on the fifth try. A Bradford Gilbert lived here, and when he was at home he could be found on the third floor. Dick noted the door number and climbed two flights of stairs to reach it.

There was no response to his prolonged prodding at the bell push and he knew a bitter nagging of defeat. Why couldn't he look the facts of life straight in the eye and admit he was horsing around to no avail?

He was walking towards the staircase again when a girl appeared. She strode purposefully along the passage until she lifted her head suddenly and saw him. He caught a flicker of alarm in her wide-eyed gaze as she came to an abrupt halt, then wheeled as though to dash back down the stairs.

'Excuse me,' he said quickly.

'Yes...' She halted and turned to look at him and he saw that she was fair and slim and extremely pretty. He mustered a relaxed smile to his face.

'I hope you won't think me impertinent, but were you intending calling on Mr. Gilbert?'

'That – that's right,' she stammered, colour creeping into her cheeks. She went on rapidly and with more confidence. 'I'm a friend of Brad's. You don't have to tell me you are a policeman, because I can see that you are.'

'Now what do you know!' Dick beamed disarmingly. 'Has it come to the stage where it really shows through?'

She laughed shakily and took a step towards him. Even if he was a policeman he was handsome and quite human, she thought. Still, she couldn't help wondering why he was trying to find Brad.

'You are looking for Brad? Don't tell me he's in some kind of trouble...'

'Of course he isn't. Not that I know of, anyhow. I did want to have a word with him, though. Have you any idea where he would be as he isn't at home?'

She shook her head.

'My name is Myrna Stewart. I've been seeing Brad a lot, on and off, if you see what I mean.'

'I do see what you mean. Then you didn't have a date with him for tonight?'

'No, not exactly. I came here merely on the chance of him being at home. He was out of work and he told me he was in the process of finding another job.'

'Oh?' Dick produced his cigarette case and offered her one. Then he supplied a light. 'He was a trucker at one time, I believe?'

'Yes. There was some trouble. A truck he was driving was held up. Brad took a beating. He was beaten unconscious, and when he came to, the truck had vanished.'

'I heard all about it.' Dick decided it would be good psychology to admit to this, as to pretend ignorance might rouse her suspicions and set her up against him.

'There was a lot of nasty talk about him being implicated in the truck robbery,' Myrna said hastily. 'It was nothing but a bundle of dirty lies.'

'I have no reason to doubt what you say, Miss Stewart. So he is trying to land another job? Where? Here in town?'

'No, I don't think so. That was the reason he gave me for not being able to see me for a few days. He said the job would mean he would have to move out of town. But he did warn me that he mightn't be around for a while. Well... There's no sense in my hanging about waiting for him. You did ring his doorbell?'

'He isn't in his apartment,' Dick assured her.

She laughed shakily again, evidently embarrassed and a trifle anxious about her boy-friend.

'In that case I'll be on my way. You – you're sure that he isn't in trouble?'

'I haven't heard if he is,' Dick replied honestly.

'Well, goodbye for now.'

'Goodbye, Miss Stewart.' He was tempted to ask her where she lived so that he could conveniently get in touch with her later if it were necessary, but he changed his mind and watched her trip quickly to the landing. Her shoes rattled down the staircase and receded rapidly towards the street.

Puffing at his cigarette, Dick returned to ground-floor level and sought out the manager. The manager turned out to be a horsy-faced female in her mid-fifties who peered along her nose at him with disapproval.

'Yes, sir,' she said with a loud sniff. 'What can I do for you?'

'I'm a friend of Mr. Gilbert's,' Dick told her. 'I understood he was stopping here, but he doesn't seem to be in his apartment. Is there the possibility that he has checked out within the last few days?'

'That would be Mr. Gilbert on the third floor? No, he has not checked out.'

'I see. Would you know then if he has been getting home in the last day or so?'

'Come to think of it, I haven't noticed him

lately. Are you a policeman? Has Mr. Gilbert been up to something?'

'I said I was a friend,' Dick replied coolly. 'No, he has not been up to anything.'

'Then I'm sorry, but I can't help you. Maybe if you just keep calling...'

'I'll do that.'

Dick touched the brim of his hat briefly and left her. Out in the coolness of the Street he brought his underlip between his teeth in vexation. Where did he go from here, he wondered. Was there really any percentage to be gained from following up the slender case to be made out against Brad Gilbert and Roy Judge? He didn't honestly think that there was, and yet some sixth sense urged him to dig a little deeper into the activities of the pair.

Making up his mind finally, he decided he would try and get a line on the whereabouts of Judge.

He didn't have an idea as to where Roy Judge could be located, and realised with a twinge that he should have tackled Anse Weaver for this information also. Still, the night was young and he could cover a lot more ground between now and the time when he liked to roll between the sheets.

It was close to midnight when he got a whisper regarding the hoodlum's address. According to his informant, who benefited to the tune of another five dollars from his billfold, Judge was supposed to be residing in a cheap hotel not far from the centre of town.

It was the sort of joint where the desk clerk glanced all round him and over his shoulder before bending to the degree of answering Dick's query.

'A fellow called Judge? Sure, he has been living here for the past week or so. He isn't here now, though.'

'I see. When did he leave?'

'Checked out first thing yesterday morning.'

'Did he stop here on his own?'

'Yeah, he did.'

'Any idea where he planned to move to?'

'Are you kidding? Ask a guest that question and you're asking for a bunch of knuckles in the teeth.'

'I understand,' Dick nodded. 'I had the feeling it was a high-tone place the minute I crossed the lobby. Thanks anyway.'

'You're welcome, Lieutenant,' the clerk smirked.

Dick went back to his car, battling with a wave of excitement. The whole thing could fit, he told himself. Gilbert going out of town to find a job. Judge checking out of his hotel yesterday morning. Perhaps fate had guided him to that pool hall on Denver after all.

If only he could gain some kind of rapport

with Wesley Regan.

Dick drove home to his apartment on Court Boulevard with the intention of putting through a call to Regan and pleading with him to cut him in on the trouble.

The telephone bell was burring as he crossed the threshold.

'Dick Knight,' he said sharply as he grabbed the receiver.

'Dick, this is Doris. I've tried twice before to get in touch with you...'

'I'm sorry, Doris, I was out. Have you heard anything fresh in connection with Carol?'

'Not really, Dick,' the woman replied in a tense whisper. 'But there is something very fishy going on. This morning a car with guards in it arrived from the bank. I know it was from the bank because Mr. Biersly, the manager, was sitting in the back seat. They brought a cardboard carton into the house. They were all together in Mr. Regan's study for a long time. Dick, I'm certain they brought a load of money. You – you don't think–'

'Listen, Doris,' the detective interrupted her, 'just forget what you saw. I've got an idea about the whole thing. I'm working on it. Mr. Regan hasn't done anything with the money yet?'

'No. He hardly leaves his study. At the minute he's having a walk in the grounds to get some air.'

'All right, Doris. Now pay heed to this. If you suspect that Mr. Regan intends leaving the house at any time during the night, give me a ring at once.'

'Very well, Dick, I'll do as you say. But what about the morning? You might be out when he leaves and–'

'I'll take care of that angle also. But remember, not a word of this to anyone else.'

'I promise, Dick, I promise. Do – do you know what I think is going on…'

'What?' he said tersely, guessing what she would say but interested in hearing her say it.

'I think Carol has been kidnapped.'

'You do, huh? Well, you could be right, honey. But keep calm and maintain your nerve. If Wes suspects we are on to him he could blow his top and do more harm than good.'

'I see what you mean, Dick. I do trust you. Goodbye for now.'

Dick said goodbye and hung up. He stood for several seconds staring off into space, then he lifted the receiver once more and dialled a number.

'Police Headquarters?' he murmured. 'This is Sergeant Knight. Pull in Lieutenant Wills, wherever he is, and tell him I'll be along there shortly to see him.'

CHAPTER TEN

Wesley Regan was kept on tenterhooks all day on Friday. He expected at every moment of the morning to have a further call from the kidnapper. No call was made. What in hell was their game? He had been told to secure the million dollars with all possible speed. He had done that. He had succeeded in arousing Marvin Biersly's curiosity to a point where the banker could contain himself no longer. He had rung up the millionaire on his arrival back in town with his guards.

'You know I'm not a man to pry into the affairs of my customers, Mr. Regan. I work from morning until night for my customers. I give of my best and endeavour to cement and maintain happy relationships—'

'What are you driving at?' Regan demanded bleakly.

'I merely wish to extend my help, Mr. Regan, my professional advice. Any modest talent I may possess is at your disposal for the asking...'

'That's mighty nice of you, Marvin,' was Wes Regan's terse response. 'But I don't need your advice or your talents at the moment.'

'Very well, Mr. Regan. Sorry to have bothered you.'

'That's okay, Marvin,' Regan hung up.

When he had seen the extent of the bulk formed by a million dollars in ready cash he had grown alarmed and asked Biersly to hire him out a suitable safe. This had been provided with the greatest alacrity, and likely it was thought of so much money being stored in the house which had caused Marvin Biersly to put two and two together and conclude that one of his richest customers was in some kind of trouble. But the banker knew better than to raise an alarm of any nature purely on his own initiative.

By the late afternoon Wesley Regan's nerves were in a bad state. Never one to seek either courage or consolation in a bottle, he, nevertheless, found himself tippling sparingly of Scotch.

It was all part of their accursed plan, he surmised. Their first move had been to acquaint him of Carol's fate and warn him against impulsive action. Their next move had been to assure themselves of his readiness and complete willingness to make the million-dollar ransome available. Their third move was couched in devilish cunning and was calculated to make him sweat it out.

They were making a damned good job of it. He was sweating it out, and plenty. If he didn't have another communication from them soon he was certain he would go crazy with worry.

Carol ... His beautiful baby. The daughter that he loved and cherished above anything else in the world. How he had gone out of his way to advise her, to protect her! Carol had resented this, naturally. Well, it was only natural that youth should resent the restrictive directives of the elderly.

Perhaps that had proved his downfall. He had shielded her too well; he had frowned on her association with that cocky detective, Knight. He had tried to wrap her in cotton wool and the experiment had proved a failure. It would have been infinitely better had he permitted Carol to drive her own car. Then she would have had no need of Travis to depend on to carry her around. Under her own steam she would have been a free agent, and the necessity of Travis' calling for her at the Art Academy would have been obviated.

Fool, he flailed himself on the heels of this reflection. If a band of kidnappers had set her up as their victim, then they would have devised some other method of tricking her into their clutches.

He took an occasional stroll in the grounds of the big house, hoping that the fresh air would have some miraculous therapeutic effect on his tortured mind; it was not to be. There was no magic in the air. The air continued to vibrate with the dire speculations his over-active brain persisted in conjuring.

At eleven-thirty he accepted a cup of coffee from Doris Maddox. The housekeeper had a face like doom, he figured. She knew that Carol was missing and she mutely accused him by every glance and gesture of at least partial responsibility for her absence.

'Carol will be back any time,' he said with an insipid smile. 'Don't worry so much.'

'I can't help worrying, Mr. Regan. I implore you to get in touch with the police if you suspect that something serious has happened to her.'

Regan glared at the woman and felt like striking her. He controlled himself with a vast effort.

'Nothing has happened to her. You must believe me, Doris. And under no circumstances must you make a move without consulting me. You do understand what I mean?' he added ominously.

'Yes, Mr. Regan, I understand.'

Doris had made two attempts to get in touch with Dick Knight by telephone while her employer was walking in the grounds, without success. Despite the warning being issued to her she intended to keep on trying to contact the detective at every opportunity until she managed to speak to him. That carton of money had not been brought from the bank under armed guard just to replenish the petty cash. Doris saw sinister connotations to it. She was certain beyond any reasonable doubt that Carol Regan had been kidnapped. She had been tempted to get in touch with the police department and to the devil with the consequences, but then she had considered that this might endanger Carol further. Better to confide in Dick Knight and leave him to decide the best course of action.

It was around midnight and Mr. Regan was taking yet another stroll in the grounds when she called Dick's apartment and had an answer from him. It was twelve-thirty and Regan was smoking a cigar in his study when the telephone there rang.

The millionaire snatched up the receiver and spoke thickly. 'Wesley Regan here.'

'Hello, Mr. Regan...' It was a different voice this time, he realised. His heart thumped madly against his ribs. The speaker continued, 'Are you alone at the moment?'

'Yes, yes, I am! What is it?'

'Did you get the dough okay?'

'Sure I did. I said I would have it early and I did have it early. It's right here in my house, locked up in a safe.'

'How did your banker react when you asked for so much money in a lump?'

'He was curious why I wanted it, naturally. But it's my business and he understands this perfectly.'

'Think you can trust him?'

'Of course I can trust him.'

'And you haven't been talking to anyone else, I hope?'

'No, no one,' Regan's tone rose shrilly. 'Why can't you believe me? I'm ready to do anything you say. I'll take the money to any place you mention, on my own.'

'That's fine, Mr. Regan. That's just fine.'

'Then – then you have made your arrangements. Look–' he went on briskly, '–I could make a suggestion to you. As I said, the money is in a safe. The safe is in my study. You can get the layout of the house from Carol, then come at any time during the night. I'll leave the safe open. Come and take the money and nobody will interfere with you. Pick your own time, your own methods–'

'We have already picked our methods, Mr. Regan. You don't have to strain your brain on our account. Just listen and answer my questions. What have you told the staff about your daughter's disappearance?'

'I've told them she's gone off for a few days with a friend,' Regan replied hollowly. Here was one of the weak links in their plan and it was to be expected that it would worry them.

'That's just swell. Now how about the chauffeur who called at that acting joint for your daughter? Was he curious to hear what was up?'

Sweat curdled on the millionaire's brow.

'Yes, he was,' he said hoarsely. 'But I told him I'd had a call from Carol to say she had gone off with this friend and that she'd be back home soon.'

'He swallowed it?'

'Look, mister, if you knew me and if you knew my staff you'd realise that they accept what I tell them.'

'I'm glad to hear it.' The kidnapper was talking more rapidly now as though he was anxious to get off the line in case a check was being put out. 'How about the girl's boy-friend? Has he been around asking questions?'

Wesley Regan thought his heart was about to give up on him. Were they not aware that Carol's boy-friend was a detective-sergeant on the Kentburg force? But no, they mustn't know this. It just went to show you, they figured they had wrapped up all the angles and missed out on Dick being a police officer.

'As a matter of fact he has called,' he heard himself answer slowly and calmly. 'I had to give him the same story that I gave the staff. He was put out a little, but I've got no reason to believe he doubted anything I said.'

'I'm glad to hear that too. Okay, Mr. Regan, just sit tight and maintain your cool. Your daughter is well and safe. You'll be hearing from me again soon.'

'But wait, I—'

There was a sharp click at the other end of the line that told him the kidnapper had broken the connection. His knuckles knotted on the instrument he was holding until they whitened. His breath came and went in shallow, agonised gasps.

'The bastards,' he panted hoarsely. 'Why can't they take the money at once and let Carol go free? What are they waiting for? What are they planning? Why are they keeping me hanging on the hook?'

He slammed the receiver down on its rest, bent across his desk and cupped his hot face in his trembling hands.

Dick, he thought now, like a man ready to grasp at any hope in the world, no matter how slim. Should he not take Dick into his confidence and tell him the whole woeful tale? As things stood he was certain that Dick believed his daughter to have been abducted. Even without having to be asked, would Dick take it into his head to pass on his fears to headquarters? But no, he wouldn't do that. He had said he would make no move whatever which could entail danger being directed at Carol.

All the same, a cop was a cop, and there

was no telling how his cop's brain would operate in such a situation.

At twelve-thirty Dick Knight was drawing up at the dimly-lit front of the building housing Police Headquarters. A minute later he was making forced small-talk with the sergeant holding down the desk.

'I put in a call to lay on the lieutenant,' he said briskly at length. 'He hasn't arrived yet?'

'Sure he has, Dick. He's along in his office right now, waiting for you.'

'Why the hell didn't you tell me so?'

'Why the hell didn't you ask me?' Sergeant Grenson retorted with a malicious chuckle. 'I figured you were on vacation or something. Can you not live without the job?'

Dick went on back into the corridor without answering Grenson.

Lieutenant Jim Wills, forty years of age and six feet of big bone and hard muscle, was puffing unenthusiastically at a cigarette when he knuckle-rapped the door of the office and walked in. Wills had been perched on the edge of a cluttered desk, striving with his impatience, and now he slipped off it, stifling an exaggerated yawn.

'What have you picked up in your coffee?' he said to Dick. 'I thought they had given you a few days off to gather rosebuds and find out what living is all about. Did the exercise pall on you too soon?'

Dick Knight and the lieutenant had worked together successfully on numerous cases. A mutual respect for each other's qualities and capabilities existed between them. Dick thought of Wills much as he might have thought of an older brother, always taking great care never to invite situations in which an elder brother could be forgiven for administering an admonitive kick to the seat of his pants.

Whilst reluctant to take anyone into his confidence at this delicate stage, he did need help, and he believed it could be supplied by Wills in the context of the secrecy he considered was essential.

'I'm in a sticky spot, Jim,' he said bluntly. 'I could use a little semi-official co-operation.'

'Oh? That does have intriguing overtones. Sit down, Dick. Tell me all about it.'

'First of all, I must have your promise that you won't expand what I'm going to tell you beyond the limitations which I lay down, Jim.'

'Uh-huh! That kind of stuff? Okay, Dick, I don't have a five-cent clue as to what's bugging you, but I do get the general drift regarding it being some kind of top secret. Go ahead and cry on my shoulder.'

Dick told him everything that had occurred from the moment he realised that Carol

Regan had been kidnapped. Wills listened silently until he was through. By then the lieutenant's eyes had an animated glitter.

He stood in front of Dick, taut with readiness to move into immediate action.

'And you want to keep this quiet?' he demanded on a sharp note of urgency. 'Are you out of your mind, Dick? It's obvious to me that your girl-friend is the victim of a kidnap plot, despite what Wesley Regan says. And just because old Wes is frightened stiff there is no reason for pandering to his ideas or whims. A kidnapping is police business, Dick. I don't have to spell it out for you. Let me put the machinery into movement at once. I'll give you a guarantee that nothing will be done which might attract danger to Carol...'

'Oh, the hell with it Jim!' Dick burst out. 'You're talking from behind your badge and you know it. I was a fool for saying a damn thing to you. So okay, go ahead and put it on the record that Carol Regan has been kidnapped. But wait and see where you get. I'll say I never told you anything of the sort. Old Wes will deny that his daughter has been kidnapped to his last breath. How silly will you look then?'

'I'm giving some consideration to the girl,' Wills retorted stubbornly. 'If we make a compact to suppress this, you understand where it can land the both of us?'

'And all the time you're considering the girl,' Dick sneered. He rose from his chair and straightened his hat. 'I'm sorry I pulled you out of bed, lieutenant. Go back home and pretend you dreamed it, huh?'

Wills pushed his fingers through his hair and sighed.

'Well, okay, Dick. You're not a fool. I know that I am. I ought to have a thorough decarb done on my thinking machine.'

'Then you will co-operate, Jim?'

'What the hell else can I do? All right, Dick, bring the rest of the fancy trick from down your sleeve. You must have worked this out in detail, I suspect.'

'I have,' Dick assured him. 'I want the feeling that you're completely primed and on tap when I ask for assistance.'

'I'm your boy,' Wills said sourly. 'Hit me over the head some more. I'm beginning to enjoy it.'

'I'd like a man to work on a parallel with me, Jim. I'd like Ross Wales for preference. You can put Ross in the picture and trust him to respect the rules of the game. We've worked in double harness lots of times. What I'd like Ross to do is this,' Dick went on, 'take himself out near the Regan house as from the earliest moment he can get there. On the minute Wesley Regan moves off on his own, Ross would follow him and see where he goes. If old Wes spotted me tailing him he would be liable to do something too silly for words. I want a plain car fitted out with a radio that will beam in on a radio fitted to my own car. That way we can keep in pretty close touch.'

'At this hour of the night, when all the technicians are either drunk or asleep?'

'Will you do it, Jim? There's a whole lot at stake.'

'You're telling me,' Wills growled. 'Okay, Dick, you're right of course and there's no time to spare. I'll get those guys on the job immediately. I knew damn well I would never be on the force for long enough to draw my pension...'

For the next ten minutes the lieutenant was busy with the telephone, rapping out terse instructions, fuming when he encountered anything that remotely resembled opposition. Finally he jammed the receiver back on its hook.

'The radio wizards are going to do a rush job on your car. They'll do a matching job on a car that Ross Wales will take – or his own. You'd better have another man besides Wales. They'll have to spell each other, you know.'

'That entails broadening the picture further,' Dick grunted and rubbed his jaw. 'How about Joe Frickling?'

'I'll not bring Joe on unless it's necessary to relieve Ross. But then, if Ross has to spend the balance of the night out at Seaway Heights, he'll be ready to be relieved come morning.'

Dick sighed. 'You're right, of course.'

'It isn't necessary to spell anything out to these fellows, Dick. They're men who do what they're told and don't ask irrelevant questions.'

'But making radio signals with me instead of headquarters?'

'Yeah, it is a little irregular. You're sure you wouldn't settle for a normal radio and have everything fed through here?'

'No, I wouldn't Jim. We do it my way or we don't do it at all.'

'You're the material that petty dictators are chiselled from. All right. I'm prepared to indulge your whims. Now, Dick, this dame you said you saw making her way to Gilbert's apartment... Myrna Stewart is her name. You should have got her address. She could be in cahoots with the kidnappers and was spying out the land for her boyfriend.'

'Maybe I should have got her name. But I don't believe she's wrapped up in any of this. In any case, I have her description should it be necessary to get in touch with her later. Also,' Dick continued, 'I'm merely backing a wild hunch where Gilbert is concerned. He could be clean.'

'Perhaps. But Judge hasn't been clean since he was a babe in arms. I'd say your hunch isn't so wild. The doorman, Burley, you spoke of – how did he describe the guy who called for Carol at nine o'clock?'

'I didn't ask him. I didn't want to get him steamed up and having him making with a lot of loose talk as a consequence. I spun him a tale. Anyhow, he's short-sighted.'

'It's worth a try anyway, Dick,' Wills said. 'We don't have anything on Gilbert in our records apart from his possible connection with the hijack effort on his truck.'

'It was a good effort. It came off.'

'Sure. The newspaper people took photos of Gilbert at the time he was picked up from the roadside. I'll get a photograph for you, have it enlarged for Burley to have a gander at it. If Burley can positively identify Gilbert as the joker who dressed up as Regan's chauffeur, then you will have something definite to go on.'

Dick considered the angle for a moment. Yes, he decided finally, it was a reasonably good one. But it might not be necessary to trouble the newspaper people. If he could gain admittance to Brad Gilbert's apartment there might be a photograph of him there. He explained this to the lieutenant.

Wills shook his head.

'You want the strictest secrecy for the moment. Then leave the apartment alone for the present. You'd have to ask the manager for a key. Should Gilbert return there

151

for some reason, he could easily learn that a cop was snooping. The folks at the *Gazette* won't turn a hair one way or the other.'

'I guess you're right. When could I have a photo?'

'I'll arrange it first thing in the morning. I could get it tonight, but it might raise suspicions. As soon as I receive it I'll have it delivered to your place.'

The radio technicians arrived shortly afterwards and went to work fitting up a radio to the specified requirements. Then Ross Wales turned up to see what was in the wind. Dick went out to his car while the lieutenant briefed Wales.

The radio technician told Dick what he had done.

'The radio in the other car will be beamed in on this frequency. If you wish to maintain contact while you're in your apartment you can slip it out so and carry it up. Watch me for a moment and I'll show you how to extract it and replace it.'

Dick watched closely and announced finally that he understood thoroughly.

'Well, that's that. Where is the other car?'

Dick pointed to the one Ross Wales had driven up in. The technician removed his light and his tool-kit and headed for the Plymouth sedan. Dick went inside again to tell Wales what was going on.

A short time later he and Wales tested

their radios. The reception of both was well-nigh perfect.

'I wish you guys could have told me about this earlier, Sarge. I haven't had a wink of sleep in fifteen hours.'

'You can get to bed in the morning, Ross. Joe Frickling will drive out there and give you his car to drive home in.'

'Sure, Sarge, I understand. Forget it. If Mr. Regan moves out of his house I contact you at once. The lieutenant couldn't tell what the gag is in aid of, so I don't suppose you can either.'

'You don't have to cram your head with a lot of stuff that won't matter to you, Ross. Get out there now and don't fall asleep whatever you do.'

'Be seeing you,' Wales grinned. 'I'll put a test call through as soon as I arrive. You'll be home by then?'

Dick nodded and watched while Wales drove off.

He hoped he was doing the right thing in taking the lieutenant into his confidence. But he knew he could trust Wills, and he knew too that Wales and Frickling would live up to the trust placed in them.

Dick checked with the lieutenant and then drove back to his apartment, removing the transceiver and taking it in with him.

Soon afterwards the radio bleeped and he heard from Ross Wales. The detective had

153

discovered a secluded spot where he could keep the big house under surveillance without being seen.

'That's swell, Ross,' Dick told him. 'Just make sure that you don't miss a trick.'

'Sweet dreams, Sarge,' Wales chuckled and signed off.

Dick realised that Doris Maddox could have tried to make contact with him during his absence from the apartment, but then the woman had sense enough to keep calling at intervals until she finally raised him. He waited half an hour before turning in. He slept fitfully and kept having nightmares in which Carol Regan figured prominently and tragically.

No one roused him during the remainder of the night. At seven-thirty in the morning he heard from Ross Wales again. Joe Frickling had arrived and was taking over.

'Nothing stirred at the house, Sarge,' Wales added.

'Okay, Ross. You're a pal.'

'I know. Look, if you like I can snatch a catnap, breakfast, and be on hand again if you need me.'

'Thanks, but it isn't necessary, Ross.'

At eight-thirty Dick was rapping on the door of Frank Burley's apartment once more. A special messenger had delivered a good photograph of Bradford Gilbert and the detective wished to have the doorkeeper's reactions immediately.

Burley was abed when he called and came to the door in a shapeless dressing-gown. He brought Dick inside and examined the photograph with the aid of his glasses. He scratched his head at length.

'I'm not sure. You see, the fellow in the uniform was wearing a moustache and sunglasses...'

'Oh,' Dick said, swallowing his disappointment. 'Listen,' he went on at once, 'will you be going out within the next couple of hours?'

'Hey, what's going on? I thought you said Miss Regan had lost her purse–'

'Of course she did. This guy might have stolen it. I'll be back shortly with another photograph.'

'Well, it's your time you're using, mister. Okay, I'll be here for a couple of hours. I'll be back in bed, but you can knock me up.'

Dick drove quickly to headquarters and managed to see Lieutenant Wills after a few minutes' wait.

'Burley didn't recognise Gilbert from the photo. The chauffeur was wearing dark glasses and a moustache.'

'Naturally he would have disguised himself. The moustache could be a false one, or Gilbert could have grown one since this picture was taken. Gilbert might not be your man, Dick. But we'll have a couple of artistic touches added to the photo and try Burley again. It's what you want to do?'

It was, Dick agreed. Wills ordered a rush job done on the photograph. As an afterthought, Dick suggested drawing in a peaked cap as well. The result when the touched-up photograph came through to them was amazing.

'Now he isn't Bradford Gilbert at all,' Dick murmured.

'He would have planned it so, wouldn't he? Try the doorman with this and let me know what he says. I'm taking a fatherly interest, Dick.'

Dick went back to Frank Burley and found him making his breakfast. Burley looked at the altered photograph. He nodded without hesitation. 'Sure, mister, this could be the same guy right enough,' he said.

CHAPTER ELEVEN

The girl's spirits ebbed as Friday night set in.

At the outset she had had the feeling that she would not be here in this strange house with these strange men for long. After the initial shock of being tricked and abducted she had pulled herself together in some miraculous fashion, adapted herself to the harsh shift of circumstances, and she had even found herself smiling a trifle grimly when she considered the furore that would be caused at home. It had been a little like taking a part in a play. You stepped into the skin and bones of a character and endeavoured to gauge and savour emotions and outlook that contrasted sharply with what you really did feel and see. It had been thus with Carol for a little while. She was not Carol Regan at all, but a character in a scene staged by Miss Bridges. And then the glamour had gone off the role and reality had asserted itself, chill and unsympathetic. And at last she had known fear.

What had taken place outside of this room that was her prison? she wondered. How had her father reacted on hearing she was in the clutches of those kidnappers?

Knowing her father, she was convinced he would do nothing rash, take no risk whatever that could bring danger to her. Yes, there was the element of danger present, grave danger. Men who kidnapped the relations of wealthy men were invariably hard and cruel, and would become desperate should their own hides be threatened.

If they didn't get what they wanted they might kill her. The thought had crossed her mind lightly at first, but then it had assumed proportion and menacing weight. Even if they did succeed in getting the ransom they demanded they might still kill her.

Her sole hope lay in the man called Jay. Of the four he was the only one she would trust to any degree. For the others, the fat man was grasping and heartless, the sallow-skinned man sent shivers racing along her spine, the cocky one with the shrill, mirthless laugh would molest her at the first opportunity, and might be the most dangerous of the quartet.

She had not seen Jay since lunch time. He had carried in her meal and gone off immediately, not looking at her, sullen and uneasy. She had tried to draw him into further conversation, but he refused to speak a word to her. Perhaps he regretted what he had done. Perhaps he was thinking about the offer she had held out to him. A half million dollars would be a vast fortune to such a man. Likely he dared not consider it for fear of the temptation and the possible resultant aftermath. Yes, he would be reluctant to cross the other three in any manner. If he did and was caught they would kill him.

It was the sallow-faced man who had brought in her evening meal. He just stood and stared at her for a minute, his eyes inscrutable, then he had gone from the room and slammed the bolts home.

At that stage there was daylight left in the sky. She wouldn't be bothered until morning unless she had reason to go to the bathroom.

Carol had eaten her meal and then looked up at the small window. She had drawn over a table below the window and found that by placing a chair upon it she could stand with her eyes on a level with the window and look out.

All she saw was the woods, the tall trees with a track winding through them. The bases of the trees were entangled with all sorts of undergrowth. She spied a squirrel sitting on a branch and watched it until it scurried into the higher branches. Sight of the squirrel made her more conscious of her plight.

She lowered herself at length to the table and to the floor, then arranged the furniture as it had been. She wished she had a cigarette to smoke. She thought of rapping on the door and asking the sallow-faced man for a cigarette, but she dropped the idea. He might get the notion she could be encouraged to a more friendly footing. A shudder ran through her.

At least she knew she was in the woods. On the way out of town she had attempted to memorise the twists and turns they made, but she had given up in frustration when she realised how useless the exercise was.

Why hadn't her father come through with the money? Was he holding off in the hope of the police being able to trail the kidnappers to their lair? She fervently hoped not. And Dick... Had he told Dick what had taken place? Had he taken Dick into his confidence?

'Oh, Dick,' she whispered and sobbed. 'If only you knew the state of misery I'm in right now...'

She slept sluggishly that night, dreaming that the whole thing was no more tangible than a horrible nightmare. She was back home with her father, laughing and telling him about her dream.

Kripp let her out to the bathroom in the morning. His still features offered no hint of his thoughts. He was smoking a cigarette and yawning. Her yearning for a cigarette overcame her caution.

'Could I have a cigarette, please?' she said as he escorted her along the corridor.

'Sure, here...' She was surprised when he forced a half pack on her. It gave her the courage to put a question to him.

'Is – is my father willing to pay you the money you're demanding?'

'Please, Miss, no slack talk, no pack drill.'

She lowered her head and entered the bathroom, closing the door behind her. She remembered that the man hadn't given her a light. On her way back to the bedroom she requested a light. He flicked a lighter and returned it to his pocket.

'You haven't got any matches?'

'Sorry, Miss,' Kripp said with a meagre grin. 'A fire would be one good way to attract a crowd, wouldn't it? But you might die in the blaze.'

She shuddered involuntarily and hastened to get beyond his reach and his gaze.

It was Brad who brought her breakfast.

She was pale and tense, he thought with an anxious twinge. Supposing she withered up and went sick on them? They would be in a keen fix then and no mistake.

'Hello, Jay,' she said when she had backed away from the door without being told to. 'What have you got there to eat this morning?'

'More eggs and ham,' he said shortly without lifting his eyes to her. 'Rye bread and fruit juice.'

'I don't want it,' she said suddenly, a mood inflicting itself upon her without warning.

Brad stared at her, narrowed-eyed, slightly suspicious of her as ever.

'What's the matter with you? You aren't sick?'

'Wouldn't you be sick of being cooped up here?' she rounded on him spiritedly. 'What do you take me for – a goddamn battery hen?'

'It won't be for much longer,' he said without really thinking. 'Get a grip on yourself,' he added gruffly. 'A big girl has got to eat. If the big girl doesn't eat she will be sick.'

'And you should care! If I was lying here dead you wouldn't turn a hair, would you?'

'Please calm yourself, Miss Regan.'

'Calm he says! I might as well be under sentence of death, and he tells me to be calm!'

He thought she could be putting on an act, but the way two large tears rolled down her cheeks convinced him that she wasn't. Her breath choked in her throat and impulsively he stretched out his hands to her shoulders. She recoiled in revulsion, her hazel eyes flaring.

'You lay a finger on me and I'll scream!'

'For pete's sake wrap it up,' he snarled angrily, colour flooding into his cheeks. 'The guys will think I'm doing something

162

with you.'

'Just you try!'

She reached for the bowl of sugar on the tray and brought it back to hurl at him. Then she dissolved, slumping on to a chair while her whole body shook.

'Please, Miss Regan...'

He took the bowl from her fingers and replaced it on the tray. He stood for a moment, gazing dumbly at her, then he turned abruptly to the door.

'Wait, Jay!'

He waited, his heart thumping sickeningly against his ribs, his mouth dry and sour. She raised her head and dashed the tears from her eyes.

'I'm sorry, Jay ... really, I am.'

'Forget it.'

'When are they going to turn me free?' she said shakily.

'Soon. Pretty soon.'

'When is soon? Today? Tomorrow? The day after that? Next week? Next year!'

'You'd better control yourself, Miss Regan.'

'And you'd better get some sense into your head,' Carol snapped. 'I'm not kidding, mister. You fellows think you're pretty smart, but you're not so smart at all.'

'How come?' he said bluntly, impressed by the vehemence in her tone. 'Go on and tell me.'

'All right, I'll tell you. Do you know who

my boyfriend is? Did you go to the trouble of finding out? I bet you didn't! It shows how even a bunch of smart guys like you can slip up. Well, my boy-friend is a cop, Jay. How do you like that now?'

Brad's jaw went slack as he gaped at her. She was joking, of course; she just had to be joking. She was deriving a sadistic satisfaction from scaring the hell out of him. Or maybe being confined in this way had driven her crazy, jumbled up her marbles and catapulted her into a kind of wonderland.

No, she wasn't joking: she wasn't crazy. He could tell by the manner she sucked in her breath and brought her teeth together. In the wake of her outburst she regretted what she had said. His expression sent a shaft of terror lunging through her.

'I – I–' she began with a silly laugh.

'A cop,' Brad said softly whilst his eyes danced over her face. 'What is a rich dame like you doing with a cop?'

'I – I was kidding you, Jay,' Carol said in a thin, vibrant voice. 'I said the first thing that came into my head. Well, do you blame me? If you were in my place, wouldn't you–'

'What is his name?'

'Whose name?'

'The cop's name.'

'I don't know! Look, there isn't any cop. I told you, didn't I? I was making up a story. If my father heard of me going out with a

164

policeman he would drum me right out of the family album.'

'If you refuse to tell me, you'll have to tell the fatman.'

'What!' She shuddered and moved to touch his arm. He waited for her to recoil, but she didn't. 'You would turn me over to him? But, Jay you wouldn't. I can't see you doing that...'

'Listen, sister, it's my neck too. Get it? I'm in on the fun. If your boy-friend is a cop I want you to say that he is. Then I want you to tell me his name and his rank.'

'What – how will you apply the inform-ation if I do tell you?'

'Let's hear the facts in detail first of all,' Brad urged.

'Jay,' she said tremulously, 'listen to me. You can help me and help yourself. Get me away from here and you'll receive the half million dollars I promised you. I won't go back on my word, Jay. My father will pay you willingly. He'll see to it that you have protection until you are well clear.'

He breathed shallowly as he stared down at her. She had her fingers caught in both his arms and her full, firm bosom touched his shirt front. Her wide, hazel eyes struggled with his own, full of pleading for mercy and understanding and aid.

Brad grabbed her to him and plastered his mouth hard against hers. He released her suddenly and flung her violently from him, so that she collided with a chair and finished up leaning on the bed, her hair awry, lips gleaming wetly, eyes flashing.

'So you're just like the others,' she taunted. 'You're no better than they are ... maybe you're worse. At least I know where I stand with them... His name is Richard Knight and he's a sergeant of detectives.'

'What?'

'You heard me. Go away and leave me alone. If you don't go away I'll scream.'

The room door was rapped sharply and Jack Royal thrust his head in. His gaze swept from Brad to the girl, then raced back to Brad.

'Get out of here.'

'But I–'

'Get out of here.'

When Brad was out of the room Royal slammed the door and rammed the bolts home.

'You're the guy who wanted to preserve what the dame has left of her virginity,' he sneered. Then his voice became chill. 'Have you gone out of your stupid mind, Brad?'

They went into the living-room where Kripp and Judge were sitting. All three regarded Brad with blank expressions.

'I wasn't touching her,' he said finally.

'No?' Judge said with his neighing laugh. 'What were you doing then – exchanging views on the weather?'

Brad swung to look at Royal.

'You figured you were smart, Jack. You spent months going over all the angles, planning the whole gag down to the last tiny detail–'

'What the hell are you talking about?' the squat man cut in on him. 'Did she say something to you? If she did, you can be sure she was bluffing.'

'I'm not sure that she was bluffing. What does she have to gain by bluffing? She was mad at being shut up in there and it just slipped out of her.'

'What slipped?' Kripp queried vaguely.

Brad didn't answer him. He kept on looking at Jack Royal.

'You knew she had a boy-friend?'

'Of course I knew. I told you she had a boy-friend. She went out with him two or three nights a week.'

'But you didn't trouble to investigate the guy, Jack. That's where you made your big mistake. His name is Richard Knight and he's a cop. A detective sergeant.'

'The hell he is!' This from Judge who had gone white about the mouth. 'The lousy bitch. She's spinning you a yarn, Brad, hoping to soften you, hoping to spread a panic amongst us.'

'She's a liar,' Jack Royal said thickly. 'What would a dame like her be doing keeping company with a cop?'

'So you failed to investigate the guy?' Brad gritted accusingly. 'And I thought you were a master-mind, Jack. I really did think you were a master-mind.'

'Stay here,' Royal said and left them. He was making for the girl's bedroom, Brad realised, and made a move after him. Roy Judge shifted quickly to block him.

'Easy does it, Brad. You heard what Jack said. It's possible the dame was only pulling your leg.'

'Sure,' Brad sneered. 'And again it's possible she was telling the truth. You actually came this far without bothering to go into everything? Everything?'

Judge evaded his glare.

'Jack knows what he's doing.'

'He'd better, pal. Unless he does, this is our last week of freedom. Have you weighed it up?'

It was evident that Judge and Kripp had; it was equally evident that they didn't like the picture Brad hinted at.

Royal was back shortly. He didn't seem so sure of himself now. He nodded to the unspoken question directed at him by Roy and Pete.

'I guess she was telling you the truth, Brad. The boyfriend is Dick Knight of the local police department. But there is a grain of comfort in it all. Her old man and Knight don't exactly see eye to eye. Old Wes has a thing on guys who muscle in where they don't belong. According to the girl, the cop doesn't belong in the Regan family circle.

'What you're trying to spell out, Jack, is that the cop won't pose such a danger.'

'I should have checked him out.'

'You really should, you know. But it's too late now for crying about spilled milk. Or is it?'

Royal's eyes narrowed on Brad.

'What are you driving at?'

'Well, there is enough time left to retreat, to back out of the deal, turn the girl loose, and scatter.'

'In other words you're scared, Brad?'

'I'm not too happy working with a guy who can make a slip like the one you've made.'

Royal could have hit him. He was tempted to do so, to wipe the smug look off Brad Gilbert's face. He suppressed his anger and filled his lungs with air. He shrugged.

'Okay, okay, so I deserve that, Brad. But it doesn't alter any of the essentials. We're going through with what we started, only if you feel inclined to take a powder, go ahead and do it.'

'Be your age, Jack. You can't afford to turn me loose and you know it. No, I'm in and I'm staying. But it means we're going to have to be twice as careful.'

Royal sighed his relief.

'Don't worry. We will be careful. I'm taking a drive for a while. I want to have another word in Regan's ear. I'll tell him that I know about the cop. I'll tell him what's going to happen to the dame if he turns him loose on us—'

'Nothing is going to happen to the dame,' Brad interrupted him bleakly. 'No matter what, Jack. Nothing.'

'Calm down, Brad. I'm bluffing, naturally. In any case I intend giving Regan his instructions today. We go through with the lift as planned tomorrow night. Have you guys objections to make? If you have I want to hear them. If you haven't, then we roll into action tomorrow on schedule.'

No one had any objections.

Ten minutes later Royal drove off in his car.

CHAPTER TWELVE

'I hear you,' Wesley Regan was saying hoarsely to the man at the other end of the line. 'I've got everything off that you've just told me. Don't worry. I won't let you down.'

'You'd better not, Mr. Regan. Everything depends on you. You should have told me about that cop and you didn't do it. I'm not too keen about trusting a man of your calibre. Why didn't you tell me? You were keeping him up your sleeve to top my hand?'

'No, no! How many times have I to say it? I can't help it if my daughter runs around with Dick Knight. But he doesn't know a thing. I wouldn't dare take him into my confidence. All I want is to have my girl back home again.'

'She'll be home again on one condition,' Jack Royal said dispassionately. 'That you play your part to the hilt. If you don't you'll have her death on your conscience.'

'You – you'd kill her?' The words were wrenched from the millionaire in an agonised groan.

'Let's look on the bright side,' Royal suggested. 'Now, Mr. Regan, repeat what I just said to you.'

Regan did so in a lifeless monotone.

'I'll pack the money into two suitcases. I'll drive one of the cars – not the Cadillac–'

'Which car will it be?' Royal interrupted him.

'A Buick station wagon. It will be handier for lifting the cases into. Do you know how much the money weighs?'

'I've worked it out roughly,' Royal replied. 'Each suitcase will weigh around twenty pounds if they contain ten thousand hundred-dollar bills. The numbers don't run and the bills haven't been marked with invisible ink?'

'I have obeyed your instructions to the letter,' Wesley Regan said wearily. 'Shall I continue?'

'Yeah, do. And snap it up while you're at it.'

'I'll use the Buick. It's a dark blue. I'll leave the house at eleven-thirty tomorrow night without telling anyone that I'm going. I'll take a roundabout route to the Dorton road and reach a point at a quarter mile short of the road fork at twelve. There I'll get out of my car and start walking towards Kentburg. If I'm stopped by the police I'll explain that my car broke down. But it's highly unlikely that I will be stopped...'

'It's possible,' Royal's voice droned. 'If the cops want to fix your car, let them. But don't under any circumstances remove the ignition key or tamper with the plug leads just to make it look good to the cops. When the car turns over for them you can say something about the fuel pump acting up.'

'I – I understand...' Regan was sweating. The sweat stood out on his forehead in cold beads. There was a sick, hollow feeling in the pit of his stomach. 'If all goes to plan I'll keep walking for half an hour, then return to my car and drive home. How soon after that can I expect Carol?'

'If you play the game I'll give you a call before the night is out. The call will tell you when and where you can collect your daughter.'

'Is – is that everything?'

'Just about, Mr. Regan. But listen, if you have the slightest suspicion that you're being followed, call off the deal at once, go back home and wait for a ring.'

'I understand. You can trust me completely.'

'I sure hope so, Mister. I sure hope so. So-long for now.'

There was a click and the kidnapper had hung up.

On Saturday afternoon Dick Knight risked going back to Brad Gilbert's apartment on Holbrook Street. As had been the case before, there was no response to his ring. He did not see the manager, either on his arrival or his departure. He was standing on the sidewalk, puffing at a cigarette, when he noticed the parked car. With the aid of a bunch of keys he carried he was able to get into the car. He read the name on the licence tag. Bradford Gilbert. The engine was cold and there was a coating of dust on the windshield that hinted that the car might not have been used for days.

Everything pointed to Gilbert having moved somewhere in a hurry. But if he had moved far from the apartment where he lived, would he not have needed his car? These days a man required a car if he required to go out of the house. Society had forgotten how to travel on its feet.

Dick thought a lot about the car and Bradford Gilbert's reason for leaving it parked here. Perhaps he had been told to leave it so that there would be less risk of his being traced. Perhaps Gilbert merely wanted to vanish from the scene as though he had been caught up in the air.

Still, he would have told his girl if he intended pulling out permanently. Or would he? It was really useless digging for an answer to the question.

Dick spent the remainder of the day in trying to get a lead on Gilbert or Roy Judge. It was a fruitless exercise, and at dusk he was so angry and frustrated he rang Wesley Regan's number once more.

It was Doris Maddox who took the call.

'Is Mr. Regan there, Doris?'

'Yes, he is, Dick.' The woman spoke in a low whisper which indicated that Regan was not too far away. 'He's bound to have heard the phone and he'll be here at any moment. Listen, there has been no news from Carol or about her. At least I haven't heard a thing. I asked him a dozen times when he expected Carol to return. He says she has gone off with a friend and will be back soon. Dick, I can tell you that I'm worried near to death. Have you– Yes!' Doris said suddenly in a loud voice. 'Mr. Regan has just come in. Hold on, please.'

'Okay, Doris,' Dick murmured. 'I get it.'

'Hello, Dick,' Wesley Regan growled an instant later. 'What is it now? I hope you are not pursuing that goddamned silly notion you had about Carol...'

'I'm sorry if I upset you, Mr. Regan. But I'll continue to be concerned about Carol until I know where she is and when she will be getting home.'

'Well, it won't be long,' Regan said with affected carelessness.' I had a call from her–'

'You had?' Dick broke in on him sharply. 'Say, that's just great. Did she tell you where she is?'

'She's with a friend, as I explained earlier, Dick. She didn't say which friend, but she assured me she would be home by Sunday night or Monday at the latest.'

'That is great news, sir. So I've been indulging in needless worry after all?'

Regan laughed shortly.

'It was your cop's psychology at work, Dick. But I guess I can't blame you. I'll tell Carol to ring your place as soon as she arrives.'

'Swell! Thanks, Mr. Regan. I'll be on tenterhooks until I hear from her in person.'

'I understand. Goodbye for now, Dick.'

'Goodbye, sir.'

Dick's features wore a grim expression as he hung up. He was in no doubt that Wesley Regan was bluffing to the limit. But no; not quite. He had detected a different note in the man's tone. He had heard from the kidnappers again. He really did believe that Carol would be returned to him on Sunday night or Monday morning. If this was so, then the kidnappers had planned to lift the money some time tomorrow. They would hardly go into action by broad daylight. It would happen either tonight or tomorrow night.

Whenever it did happen he would be right there, on Wes Regan's tail. Regan might have been manoeuvred into a position where he had to believe the kidnappers and accept their terms, but certainly he was not prepared to take anything they promised as gospel. Once they had the money in their hands, Carol's life would be in extreme danger. The records showed that hoodlums of this type rarely risked the danger of eventual identification by their victims.

Dick slept fitfully that night. Before turning in he had checked with Ross Wales and warned him to be on the alert, even though he knew he could trust Ross to the uttermost.

Morning came and Wales reported that nobody had moved from the big house during the night.

'It's getting the appearance of a bum steer, Sarge. You'd think the people in there were rooted to the house. Nothing goes in and out but delivery vans.'

'Delivery vans!' Dick echoed as a terrible idea struck him. 'Look, Ross, I want every delivery vehicle checked as it leaves the house—'

'But Jo is taking over shortly, Sarge...'

'Give my instructions to Joe then. Tell him to check with the drivers and make a search of the vehicles. Tell him too to make sure that these guys don't pass along the word to Regan.'

'Okay,' Wales said. 'I get you. If only you'd told me to do this at the beginning – Sarge, if I knew what you're trying to unearth it would be a help.'

'Sorry. It's somewhat personal, Ross. Just

do as I tell you.'

'You bet,' the detective replied. 'I see Joe coming along the road. I'll put him in the picture.'

Dick was grey-faced and trembling as he broke the connection. How could he have been so damned stupid!

Sunday was one long drag for him. Several times he raised Joe Frickling to make certain that the detective was on the job. Frickling got ratty with him at length.

'What do you want me to do – make up a story to keep you happy? I tell you, the joint is quiet. It's just the way a Sunday ought to be, if a guy could be at home and minding his own business.'

'I'm sorry, Joe.'

'Forget it, Sarge. I'm kidding. This gives me a good excuse to duck out on visiting with my mother-in-law. We drive to see her every Sunday, you know.'

'Really? Your Sundays must be a ball.'

'Why don't you get married and try some of the pudding for yourself? But then you wouldn't have a mother-in-law, just Daddy Billion-bucks. I envy you, Sarge.'

'I'm not married yet,' Dick said tersely. 'If I do marry it sure won't be for money.'

'I'll have a dollar on that! The wiseacres will tell you it's the root of all evil.'

Several times during the day, too, Dick

was tempted to abdicate his lone wolf act and turn the whole thing over to the department. If he did he could be assured of smooth and rapid action under the veil of the closest secrecy. He resisted these temptations, not without a twinge of guilty conscience. Were the girl anyone other than Carol Regan, he would have the strength of the department with bells on, and not think twice about it.

Dusk fell at last. Ross Wales came back on duty and Joe Frickling rode home to his wife. Dick and Ross exchanged a few words before the detective settled down to his night's vigil. There was a forced cheerfulness to Wales' manner that triggered off a mild suspicion in Dick. Had the detective finally guessed at the purpose behind the strange operation he was involved in?

There was no bed for Dick that night. He had a feeling in his bones that the suspense would not be maintained for much longer. Something just had to break, and soon. Granting that the ransom money hadn't already gone out in a delivery truck, that was. If it had and Carol had not been released, then Wesley Regan would have a lot to answer for.

Dick had made certain that his car was tanked up with gas and in complete readiness. A shoulder harness lay on the living-room table and beside it lay a loaded .38

automatic, together with two spare clips.

He prowled about restlessly, fortifying himself on cup after cup of coffee. The coffee seemed to calm him down. Every now and then he would halt before the radio he had brought up from his car. A dim red light told him the radio was functioning, and there was small chance of it going out of order.

The hours crawled past. Eight, nine, ten. At eleven some of the tension receded from his nerves. It was a blessed reaction to the keyed-up state that had ridden him all day. But if it didn't happen tonight, when would it happen? And what about Carol? How was she faring? What were her feelings and her thoughts? Would the kidnappers dare to interfere with her?

Then tension rushed in on him again at the very idea.

Calm yourself down for pete's sake. You're a cop, so you've got to think and behave like a cop.

At eleven-thirty the radio bleeped. Dick dashed to take the message.

'I'm here, Ross. What is it?'

'Might not be anything, Sarge, but I can see what could be the headlamps of a car up at the house... Yeah, it's a car right enough. It's on the move.' Wales' voice was cool and controlled. 'It's coming along the driveway to the road. Want me to follow it?'

'Sure!' Dick cried hoarsely. 'I'm going

down to my own car, Ross. Glue on to him and don't let him out of your sight.'

'Him? You mean Wesley Regan? What if it isn't Regan who is driving?'

This jolted Dick for a few seconds. He was altogether too willing to jump to the conclusion that the millionaire was leaving home in order to deliver the ransom money to the kidnappers. It might not be Regan at the wheel; even if it was, his errand may have nothing to do with the kidnappers.

'Follow the car anyway, Ross–'

'I've got another inspiration,' Wales said quickly. 'See how rapidly you can assimilate this. The car leaving the house could be a decoy to throw a possible watcher off the scent.'

That rocked Dick also.

'Where the hell are you getting these bright ideas from?' he groaned. 'You could be right...'

'The car is passing through the entrance gates now, Sarge. Yeah... It's the great white master himself driving. A station wagon.'

'Go after him, Ross,' Dick breathed. 'But don't let him suspect he's being followed. I'll resume contact with you as soon as I hit the street. Guide me on to your route and then you can drop off and leave me to it.'

'Ro-ger, Sarge!'

Dick pulled on the shoulder harness, made sure the .38 was on safety before thrusting it into the holster. The spare clips he rammed into his jacket pocket. Then, snatching up the radio, he left the apartment and headed for the street.

It was the work of a moment to anchor the radio, and when he tuned in to Ross Wales he heard a slow, conversational running commentary that tended to take the edge off his nervousness.

'Subject is angling towards the town highway. He's going at a normal speed. Careful is the word.'

'I'll make a start for the intake road, Ross.'

'I wouldn't advise it, Sarge. He may not be making for town at all.'

'Still, I would be that much closer to you.'

'Well, okay. You're the boss. You sound pretty steamed. It's your girl, Sarge, isn't it?'

'What the hell are you raving about?'

'Forgive me, Sarge. Slip of the tongue. Let it ride. I'm lying well back with three or four vehicles between me and the Buick.'

'Don't lose him, Ross.'

'Quit worrying... He's gathering speed. He just pulled out and passed a crawler. The crawler must be doing forty-five to fifty.'

'How far from where you are to the turnoff?'

'A brace of miles, I guess.'

'I'll make my way towards it.'

'Suit yourself,' Wales rejoined tonelessly.

Dick set his car to motion, battling with the

waves of excitement that persisted in assailing him. He knew he ought to be calm and clear-headed. As a cop he never had to remind himself of this. He didn't feel like a cop tonight; he felt like the victim of a hideous nightmare. Soon he would be climbing stairs with no end, stairs that spiralled into a dark void. Then he would be swimming in filthy water where there was a strong tide hammering him backwards. Those were the major features of his nightmares. A head-shrinker could explain their source, perhaps.

He brushed chill sweat from his brow.

'He's dropping on to the turnoff, Sarge.'

'Blazes! You should have let me start driving earlier.'

He expected and deserved a sharp retort from Wales. All the detective said was, 'Well, we can't read his mind, can we...'

'He's making for the town centre, Ross.'

'Correction,' Wales breathed tautly. 'We're travelling along St. Mark's Avenue. That's a bypass that could throw him to the far end of town. Look, Sarge, he's leaving the coast road and intending picking it up again at the south side.'

'You could be wrong. I'm going to drive fast and overtake you, Ross. Just keep talking, will you.'

'You're going to have to crash a few lights, buddy.'

Dick drove speedily but with infinite care.

His thoughts were racing on ahead of Ross Wales' patter. Where would Wes Regan be going if he hit the coast road again? Dorton? Yes, it was possible. He couldn't visualise the kidnappers holding Carol right here in town.

Wales' instructions continued to guide him. He took a gamble and cut through a section of derelict buildings and back alleys. If his hunch was correct he would save time and mileage. He kept the detective apprised of his movements.

'Looks like you could be right, Sarge. We're on Dover Boulevard and Mr. Regan is pushing the throttle.'

'Don't lose sight of him, Ross.'

Ten minutes later, his sweaty shirt sticking to his back, he was practically in Ross Wales' slipstream. And five minutes after that he was within sight of the detective's rear lights.

'I've made it, Ross. I'm going to pass you.'

'Go ahead. The best of luck. Listen ... suppose I head back to the big house anyway and stay there till you call? You don't want me with you?'

'No, thanks. Yeah, good idea. Go back to the house. I'm going to sign off for a while. If you want to raise me, do so.'

Ross Wales acknowledged and Dick sent his car surging past him. Ahead, in the distance, he saw the Buick station wagon.

CHAPTER THIRTEEN

Brad, Jack Royal and Pete Kripp left the Pine Lake cabin at eleven o'clock. Brad and Royal rode in Royal's car while Pete Kripp drove the one Roy Judge had used. They had two cars between them all, which wasn't such an attractive idea to Brad. He would have preferred his own car on hand, as it would have given him the feeling of a certain independence and mobility. The way things stood, too, Roy Judge and the girl might as well be marooned in the cabin if a situation arose where Roy needed to pull out in a hurry.

Brad didn't care for the notion of Judge and the girl being left alone at the cabin. At the very last moment he had been on the verge of objecting to the arrangement. However, had he done so a row might have followed, and at this stage of the game any kind of friction could prove disastrous. He had just spoken to Judge before leaving him.

'See you watch that girl good, Roy. And no manner of monkey trick for the sake of amusement.'

'Who do you think you're talking to?' Judge had retorted with his neighing laugh.

'Maybe you were hoping to be left holding the fort while the rest of us risked our necks.'

Judge stood at the front of the cabin and listened to the sounds from the car engines dwindling and fading. Royal had told Pete to start out ahead of him; then, a few minutes later, Jack and Brad had gone after him.

The woods were still and quiet. Only a gentle breeze drifted up through the trees from the lake. The sky was a huge velvet cloak on which the stars glittered like so many fiery diamonds.

Judge lit a cigarette and remained at the door until it was smoked down to a butt. The butt he dropped to the porch and ground beneath his heel. He was thinking of a lot of things – sunny skies and golden beaches; a big house with its back to the mountains and its front to the sea. A sleek limousine and a guy in a natty uniform to drive him around. He would sit up there with a fat cigar in his fingers and a beautiful dame at his side, squinting along his nose at the common herd. Boy, how he would tramp on the riffraff! He would show them that Roy Judge was someone to be reckoned with. In the winter there would be cruises. He would visit all the countries he had ever dreamed of visiting. There would be dames too. The world would be a grey flat plane without dames. It was dames who put the spice into life.

Something began crawling to the surface of his consciousness.

He tried concentrating on the dough instead. A million bucks. Divided into four juicy slices. The trouble was they might not get the money. There could be a slip-up that would turn the golden dream into a pitch-black nightmare. Old Regan might pull a trick on them. There could be cops swarming over the Dorton road like flies.

Royal had told him what to do if they didn't return to the cabin before morning. If they didn't turn up it could mean they had run into a trap and been killed or forced to scatter to hell and gone like frightened rabbits. If this occurred the girl would become a massive liability. So what he had to do was kill the girl and set the cabin on fire. After that he would be on his own. He would have to hoof it through the woods, get as far away from the scene as possible, hitch a lift when the opportunity arose, and continue travelling.

All these reflections stank of defeat, and whilst Judge didn't want to take a morbid interest in the black side, it had to be faced nevertheless and considered.

He was pretty sure that Jack would swing the trick successfully. Their great strength lay in the affection Wes Regan had for his daughter. Unless the millionaire was an utter fool he wouldn't dare attempt a move that would endanger the girl.

Little did he realise what Royal had planned for her. Once the money was in their possession it would be split four ways and Brad Gilbert would be sent packing. Pete would drive Brad to a town on over the mountains and drop him there to fend for himself. The girl would be speedily silenced, the cabin set alight, and then Jack and he would make their way back home to Kentburg. When the cops eventually got to weaving they would never dream of suspecting two guys who had never stirred an inch from Jack's house at Swift's Beach. Darla would be there to swear to anything which her brother put in her mouth.

Judge went inside at last, closing the door and going through to the living-room where he unearthed a bottle of whisky. Always a sparing drinker, he nevertheless felt the need of a jolt to stifle his worry. He took a stiff jag and then followed it with another. He began making dream-stuff once more on the strength of the quarter million bucks that was almost within kissing distance.

A loud hammering caused him to push the bottle and glass aside.

What the hell was the matter with her?

It was possible she wished to pay a visit to the john.

He went to the door of Carol's bedroom

and called in to her. 'What is it, baby?'

'Open up,' she said in a shrill voice.

'Okay, okay. Don't bust a seam.'

He threw the bolts back and twisted the door handle. The door came against the inner lock and he told her to release it.

Carol did so. She opened the door a few inches and stared at him.

'Oh,' she panted then. 'I – I thought it was Jay.'

She would have slammed the door on him had he not jammed his foot in the opening. A hard push sent her reeling back across the floor. Judge went inside and shut the door behind him. The girl shrank from him, eyes wide with fright, her breathing fast and shallow.

'I heard cars leaving,' she said weakly. 'I wondered what was going on.'

'You did, huh? You figured that everybody had left but Jay. And where do you get this Jay stuff? His name is Brad. Don't you know that?'

Judge was smiling and his voice was soft and friendly. The overall effect seemed to lessen the girl's fear of him.

'Brad?'

'Sure,' Judge grinned. 'Brad Gilbert. You take him for a big-shot, don't you? Well, he's anything but a big-shot, ma'am. He's the sort of specimen you wouldn't glance twice at if you were driving past him in the street in your swell Cadillac.'

'Please...' she said, shuddering. 'I'm not really interested in him.'

'Why should you be? He's nothing but a trucker, an ex-trucker to be accurate. His truck was hijacked and the cops thought he might have been mixed up in it.'

His manner was suddenly puzzling to the girl. She sensed dark, ominous undertones. She repressed another shudder. His eyes were leaping over her, lingering on the swell of her bosom, the ripe full curve of her hips, dancing to her feet and up again to her face. He laughed like a neighing horse.

'Why – why are you telling me this?'

'Why shouldn't I, baby? A guest usually cares to know the kind of company she's keeping. You were going sweet on Brad, I take it?'

'Sweet!' Her laugh was scornful. The sound of it in her ears helped her gather her reserves of courage. It would be a mistake to allow this man to see weakness in her. She must be strong, or if she couldn't be strong she must pretend to be. 'Where have the rest of them gone?' she went on sharply. 'For how much longer are you going to keep me here?'

'Not for much longer, baby.'

He took his cigarettes from his pocket, offered her one. She shrank a little further back from him and shook her head.

'Thank you, I don't want to smoke.'

Carol's brain began working swiftly. The man before her was a specimen of a breed she knew well enough. He had a smattering of intelligence, but only a smattering. Basically he was cunning and avaricious. He was involved in the kidnapping for the amount of money he hoped to get out of it. All right then, why not put out the bait she had extended to Jay – or Brad?

'Listen,' she said hastily before her better sense urged her the exercise would prove abortive, 'how much money do you expect to get as your share of the ransom?'

'Hey, hold on, my beauty!' Judge chuckled. 'You're not supposed to concern yourself with our welfare.'

'Don't worry. I'm not in the least concerned. But I can offer you a better return than you're liable to get for your share. If you help me to get out of this mess, take me and return me to my father, I promise you that my father will pay you the sum of half a million dollars...'

'Whew !' Judge ejaculated. 'You make my head swim, doll. You really do. A whole half million peanuts? And I'm sure your daddy would guarantee me a safe passage out of the country?'

'Of course he would. I promise you he won't even mention your name to the police, much less set them upon you.'

Judge pretended to think it over for a moment.

He grinned evilly at the girl.

'I just hate to disappoint you, Miss Regan. Yeah, I do, believe it or not. A half million is a lot of loot, sure, but what could I do with it after my pals got through with me. They'd catch me, no matter where I went or how fast I ran. You think I'm only kidding you? But I'm not kidding, you know. Jack Royal is a tough cookie. When he tells a man to do a thing he has got to do it or suffer the consequences.'

'Then you are afraid of him.' She tried to make it sound like a sneer but the effort did not quite come off. Her cheeks coloured and she caught her underlip between her teeth.

'Everybody is afraid of Jack, Miss Regan. If they understand what's good for them they jump when he shouts.'

'You won't help me – even for a half million dollars?'

'I'm sorry, baby. Truly sorry.'

He took a step that shortened the space between them and in that instant Carol Regan got a glimpse of what was on his mind. It made her blood curdle and panic rushed in on her.

There was a narrow gap separating Judge from the wall at his side and the door behind him. In a split second the girl came to a decision.

With a harsh cry she darted for the gap and the door beyond.

She never reached it. Roy Judge stretched out an arm to block her and she reeled off the arm to lose her balance and fall to the floor.

Judge gripped her roughly and hauled her to her feet. His face was livid and a wild light glittered in his eyes.

'You crafty little bitch,' he choked.

Carol struggled to release herself.

'I'm – I'm sorry. Please let me go and I won't do it again. Please!'

'You're damned right, you won't...'

The feeling of her ripe body snapped against him was too much for Judge. To hell with it, he thought crazily, she isn't going to get back home alive anyway, so why should I worry. And, boy, what a piece she is. What a goddamned lovely piece she is.

Carol shrieked when his strong fingers dug into her blouse. He slashed her across the mouth with his open hand and she lay heavily on him, groaning, choking words from her throat to her tongue.

'No, no... Please don't! I'll promise you anything, give you anything...'

Tears streamed down her cheeks.

Sight of them set Judge's lust on fire. He dragged her to the bed and flung her down on it. His fingers had ripped her blouse and a full breast sagged loose from her brassiere.

He buried his hot face in the soft flesh, wave after wave of exhilaration raging through him.

Once more the girl fought to release herself, and then, realising that all was lost, she closed her eyes and ground her teeth and wished herself dead and forgotten.

Judge's leaping fingers tore at her dress like searing brands. His knee drove into her thigh.

Out on the Dorton road Dick contented himself with keeping the rear lights of Wesley Regan's car in the near distance. There wasn't much traffic going to and fro at this hour of a Sunday night. In a way it was an advantage; in another way it aggravated the risk of Regan realising he was being tailed.

He must be heading for Dorton, Dick thought, fingering a cigarette to his lips and flicking his lighter beneath the tip. A lot of tension had left him now. The suspense and the waiting were over and in a short time he might get a glimpse of the kidnappers.

Dick had no clear-cut plan of action. It would simply be a case of remaining on the alert with his eyes peeled and prepared for whatever eventuality which might arise.

A mile further on the unexpected happened.

There was a car cruising in front of the detective and suddenly a vehicle travelling from the opposite direction went out of control and slithered over the road directly into its path.

There was a high-pitched screaming of brakes, followed by a dull thump. Then metal was clanging about on the road as the two cars went into a weird, frightening spin.

Dick had been going for his brakes from the instant the oncoming car lights started acting erratically, but even so his own vehicle came to rest within mere inches of the tangled mass. It meant that the road was practically blocked.

He was tempted to hunt for an opening so that he could continue his pursuit of Wesley Regan, but a twinge of conscience stopped him. Supposing that someone was seriously injured in the crash?

Choking back a curse of frustration, he climbed out and hurried forward to investigate the mess. As though by magic other cars converged on the scene by the dozen.

Their drivers parked at random, regardless of the additional hazard they were posing. A traffic accident seemed to attract the rubber-necks from every point of the compass.

Dick hauled open the door of the car that had been cruising in front of him. It was a Citroen and there was no one in it but the driver. He sat there, stupefied, eyes gaping at Dick from the back of thick-lensed glasses.

'Are you okay, mister?'

'Yeah ... I think so... That guy must be a maniac. Did you see how he swept over the road?'

'I saw.'

'The bastard must be crazy.'

'He might have had a blowout.'

Dick made his way to the second car involved in the crash. It was a Packard and it had been reduced to scrap in the impact. The driver had emerged. He was a big, stout man, hatless, and was waving his arms in the air. A small crowd surrounded him. Just then Dick heard the shrill wail of a siren and turned to see a motor-cycle rushing up. More traffic was grinding to a standstill.

'This man is drunk!'

'I'm not drunk, I tell you. Leave me alone, wilya, or I'll take a poke at ya...'

Dick snatched at the stout man's sleeve. His breath reeked of alcohol. He pushed him to the side of the road.

'Take your hands off me, ya punk.'

'You dirty soak,' Dick snarled and hung a wicked blow to the man's chin. He staggered and was caught by a few of the bystanders. 'Anyone else in that car?'

'No, there isn't. Are you a cop?'

The patrol bike came to rest and the rider shut off the siren. He was a big, blocky character and he moved in beside Dick.

'Were you driving one of these heaps, buddy?'

'I'm Detective Sergeant Knight of the city police department,' Dick told him. 'Kentburg, that is. Look, nobody is seriously injured and I'm in a hell of a hurry. Could you get me through?'

'Which direction, Sarge?'

'I'm making for Dorton.'

'Get into your car and follow me. Then I'll put in a call for help. Jezz, these morbid sightseers bug me. Listen, everybody, you're not at a circus. Anybody who didn't witness the accident take off. And that is an order.'

'This guy is drunk, Officer.'

'Give me a minute.'

A cold sweat layered Dick as he got behind the wheel and the patrol cop cleared a path for him. Once out of the mass of people and cars he tramped his shoe on the gas pedal, surging off into the direction which Wesley Regan had taken.

There was every chance now he would lose all trace of Regan. What a cursed stroke of luck.

He travelled flat out for a few miles, then, catching up with traffic once more, he was forced to slow down in order to distinguish the station wagon when he overtook it.

The man walking on the roadside registered only on the extreme edge of his consciousness at first. The man was wearing an overcoat and hat and was walking with his head down. Dick's car raced past him. Then his subconscious began feeding back pictures and he held his breath.

That man was Wesley Regan! The Buick must have stalled.

Even as the truth hit him, Dick noticed the station wagon drawn in from the main highway. He reacted immediately, stabbing at the brake; still, he was fifty yards past the Buick before he managed to come to a halt. Then, not pausing to consider all the consequences that might attend his action, he put his car into a tight U-turn, cutting across a driver who pumped his horn at him and cruising back towards the station wagon.

He was twenty yards short of the parked vehicle when he spotted a man opening the driving side door. It was one of the rare moments when the detective was ever caught flatfooted. His instinct seemed to take over automatically. He sent his car storming on to the Buick, picking up the man beside it in his headlamps. The man froze, then wheeled.

Flame erupted from his hand and the windshield of Dick's car was sundered with a million cracks, much as a section of ice will shatter under too heavy a weight.

CHAPTER FOURTEEN

Brad could hardly believe it was happening.

Right up to this moment everything appeared to be ticking over like a scene in a well-rehearsed play. Wesley Regan's station wagon had arrived at just one minute past the scheduled time. He and Jack had watched him drive the Buick on to the shoulder, get out and walk away as he had been instructed to do. They had watched the millionaire trudge out of sight and then, the coast apparently clear, Royal had touched Brad's arm and told him to move into action.

Now here he was, the whole damned picture slipped out of focus, disaster hovering above him like the shadow of doom.

Brad had made certain the station wagon was empty of hidden passengers; he had noticed the two suitcases in the back, and then that car which had gone by had slewed into a curve and raced down on him.

He drew his gun instinctively, took quick aim at the charging car, and fired.

The car continued to rock across the road towards him. It was going to smash into the station wagon, he was sure, and he ran round to the front of the vehicle.

The car missed the Buick by inches, lunged on towards seawards, and Brad's heart skipped a beat as he waited for it to rush on off the rocks and drop the hundred or so feet into the ocean.

Instead, the car struck a boulder, catapulted backwards and skywards before coming to a shuddering rest.

Brad froze for an instant in blank indecision. Then his thoughts unlocked and he sprinted to the wrecked car, gun at the ready to pump more slugs at it. He grazed his shin on a rock and almost fell. He gathered himself upright and limped on to the wreck.

The driving side door was open and the driver lay back on the seat, face white as a sheet except for a bubbling of blood creeping from his forehead. His eyes were closed and he had likely broken his neck.

A cop for sure. That lousy two-timing Regan!

Brad pointed his gun at the cop and his finger tightened on the trigger. He couldn't bring himself to complete the pressure. Other thoughts crowded in on him. Holy hell, what was he doing here? It was the money that mattered and the money might be in those suitcases, despite Regan's efforts at a double-cross. At any moment too, there would be a score of cars drawing up at the scene.

He dashed back to the station wagon, limping to favour the injured ankle. Where was Kripp, he wondered in a blaze of terror. If Kripp didn't do his stuff... But he still had the station wagon. Sure! If the keys were in the ignition.

A car was roaring from the fork towards him. It slithered in to a frantic halt and Pete Kripp leaped out.

'Jump in quick, Brad.'

'The money,' Brad snarled.

'It isn't there. He played a goddam trick...'

'Two suitcases are there. Get them.'

He reached into the rear of the Buick and hauled one of the cases over. Kripp slung it into the back seat of his car. Brad grabbed the other one, shouting furiously as he did so.

'Get behind the wheel.'

Kripp charged on to the driving seat. Brad flung the second case after the first, then slammed in beside Kripp. A car was slowing off to avoid hitting them.

'Come on, Pete. Rattle your damn hocks.'

If Brad was enmeshed in the throes of excitement, Pete Kripp was cool and clear-headed. The man fed gas to the engine, swinging his vehicle into an arc, missing another oncoming car by a hairsbreadth. He roared away at breakneck speed to the road fork.

Ten minutes went by before Brad recovered

201

a measure of calm. All this while he had been staring straight ahead of him, not really seeing the narrow road that swam past the windshield. Kripp drove fast and expertly.

At length he fed a cigarette to his lips.

'Have you got a light?'

The fingers holding Brad's extended lighter trembled badly. He caught his wrist with his right hand in an effort to shield his nervousness from his companion. Pete Kripp didn't seem to notice.

'What do you think is in them, Brad?'

'The suitcases? Bundles of old news-papers, I bet,' he said bitterly. 'That bastard deserves to be drawn and quartered.'

'Regan?'

'Who the hell else?'

'There was a guy in the car?'

'Well, there must have been,' Brad snapped. 'It didn't just come along by itself.'

'Cop for sure. You fired at him.'

'Yeah, I did. He put me into a sweat. He must have broken his lousy neck, and serve him right.'

'We're in a rare fix, pal.'

Brad glanced at the man's sallow face. Yes, they were, he realised with a sickening shock. And if those suitcases were stuffed with nothing more valuable than paper they would have gone through the agony for sweet nothing.

On top of that there was the girl. What to

do with her now that the heat was on? Brad didn't know. He had never been in such a jam in the whole of his life. Perhaps Royal would be able to think of something. Royal was the brains of the outfit, wasn't he? Well, let him figure it out. It was his baby and he'd better be up to the situation.

'What will Jack do now?' he heard himself saying.

'He'll do what he said he would do – make his way back to the cabin. But he's going to have to move fast to get clear. I'd say that section is alive with motorists by this time.'

Both men fell silent for a while. Brad couldn't help keening his ears for sounds of pursuit. No matter how hard he forced himself to relax he discovered it was well-nigh impossible. He had used his gun on a man. That gun was snugged in his jacket pocket at this minute. A killer weapon. But no, he hadn't actually shot the man. Had he? He knew he had triggered at the windshield of his car. That blood on the cop's forehead... Had it came from a gunshot wound? Was the cop Carol Regan's boy-friend?

He was a killer...

'No,' he whispered fiercely. 'I'm not.'

'What are you talking about, Brad?'

'Nothing.'

'You're shaky.'

'Blazes I'm shaky,' he retorted. 'I got the cute end of the job, didn't I?'

'I'd have been shaky myself, pal. I am shaky. This is big stuff for us. Jack has been having big dreams for quite a spell now.'

'He knows to stay in the background.'

'You tell him so.'

'I'll tell him so. You want to make something of it, Pete?'

Kripp gave an uneasy laugh.

'No, I don't, Brad. If I'd a medal I'd pin it on your shirt.'

Brad wasn't sure whether he was sneering at him. He didn't really care much. Their sentiments regarding each other were insignificant when placed against the overall picture.

Brad realised Kripp was driving through streets. He stared out of the window.

'Where are we?'

Kripp laughed again.

'Kentburg,' he said. 'I have the feeling we might be getting along nicely, Brad.'

Brad said nothing more until they were leaving the suburbs of Kentburg and angling for the Bridgeport highway. He settled a cigarette between his lips and lit it. Most of the weakness had gone from his fingers.

'We could be two rich men, Pete.'

Kripp threw him a brief look.

'On two suitcases filled with waste-paper? I should smile.'

He saw a lay-by ahead and nosed the car off the highway on to it. Brad grabbed for the gun in his pocket.

'What's bugging you?' he said hoarsely.

'I just want to see what's in them, Brad.'

'Are you nuts?' All the same, Brad was as keen as Kripp to investigate the contents of the suitcases.

Kripp stalled and killed his headlamps. Traffic on the highway scuttled to and fro. Brad got on to his knees and lugged one of the suitcases to him. It might be locked, and if it was they weren't going to dally until they forced it. He thrust the twin catches off and pulled at the lid. The lid opened. He saw neat bundles in the dim light. His blood ran thick as he lifted one of the bundles and held it closer to his face while he flipped through it.

'Money,' he panted. 'Hundreds.'

'Try some of the others,' Kripp said tensely. 'The top layer might be a bluff.'

The top layer wasn't a bluff. Each of the bundles contained bills. Wesley Regan had come through as he promised he would. But if he meant to keep his word, then where had the cop appeared from?

He just had to be the dame's boy-friend.

'It would keep us in clover for the rest of our lives, Brad.'

The urgent note in Kripp's voice did not escape Brad. He swivelled his head to peer at him.

'Just the two of us, Pete?'

205

'We might get away with it where four of us might stumble over each other.'

'Don't tempt me, man. I'd do it in a minute.'

'Say the word, Brad,' Kripp whispered, running his tongue across his lips.

A half a million bucks each, Brad marvelled. The feeling he had was too fantastic to describe. Talk about those stories of the Arabian Nights!

But wait. Perhaps he was travelling too rapidly for his own good. Here was Kripp evincing his willingness to pull a fast one on Royal and Judge. A man who would play a dirty trick on two of his friends would have few qualms about playing it on three of his friends. Apart from this consideration there was the welfare of the girl to be taken into account. He had promised that no harm would come to her. He could never look at himself in a mirror again if he didn't live up to his promise.

He tossed the money back and fastened the lid of the suitcase.

'Nothing doing, Pete. You can push your luck too far. Mine suits me fine as it is. Get going for the woods.'

Their greed and their separate reactions to it laid a strain between them for a while. Kripp soon flung his mood off. He began to whistle.

'Oh, cut that out,' Brad complained. 'It's

like dancing at somebody's funeral.'

'The Irish do it.'

'The Irish are a bunch of nuts. I hope Jack makes it okay.'

'Jack will make it.'

'I hope that cop doesn't die.'

'So what if he does die? If he had shot you first you would be the guy to die.'

'He didn't shoot at me.'

'Aw, wrap it up, Brad. You sure know how to be the life and soul of a party. With a quarter million under your belt!'

'Yeah!' Brad said in a low voice.

'Yeah,' Kripp echoed. He threw his head back and laughed. He laughed so hard Brad had to reach over and grab the wheel to keep him from driving into the ditch.

'You stupid bastard, Pete. Keep your mind on your driving.'

'Quit worrying, you warmed-up zombie. You can't even tell when the sun is shining.'

Kripp started laughing again. The reckless note of his laughter triggered off a spark in Brad. He began to laugh as well. They laughed like a couple of lunatics while the car rolled from one side of the road to the other.

They were amazed to see Jack Royal's car parked in the shadows at the cabin when they reached it. Royal must have taken a shorter route to the hills than they had.

The door of the cabin opened and the squat man stood there for a moment. He had a gun in his right hand, but when he recognised the pair he thrust it into his hip pocket and hurried out to meet them.

'Well,' he said hollowly, 'how did it go?'

'Exactly as you planned it,' Kripp cried expansively.

'Almost,' Brad amended soberly.

'You mean he was actually carrying the money?'

'Sure he was, Jack. Come and see for yourself.'

'Pull yourself together, you punk,' Brad growled.

'We're not in the clear. Get the suitcases inside.'

Brad didn't notice the look Royal slanted at him, but even if he had noticed he wouldn't have cared. A lot had happened to Brad since leaving the cabin. He had been thrust past the point of no return in his own estimation of events and his relation to them. He had killed a man, or at least caused the death of a man. The idea created a clash of chemicals within him. Depression struggled with a strange explosive exhilaration, and he had no way of judging what the ultimate result would be. Killing in a war was one thing, but killing in a sane, civilised context was a different thing altogether.

They took the suitcases into the living-room and dumped them on the table. Judge came into the room behind them and stood breathing heavily at Brad's shoulder. Brad glanced at him.

'What about the girl?'

'The girl? Is that all you can think of, you chump? You figure I would open the cage and let her fly free?'

A low whistle from Jack Royal caused them to rivet their attention on the suitcase which the squat man had opened.

'Money!' Judge croaked. 'It is absolutely real, folks?'

'It's real enough,' Royal said tersely. 'My, oh, my! You certainly did your stuff, Brad.'

'Yeah,' Brad said without feeling. 'It nearly went wrong.'

'It was a team effort and don't you forget it, Jack,' Pete Kripp murmured. 'Have a look at the other case.'

They did so, standing around, mute and bug-eyed and worshipping the money. Even Brad was impressed beyond anything he had ever experienced. What he had to do was get his share quickly and cut out and away from these characters. He thought briefly of Myrna but pushed the memory of her roughly aside. From now on he was travelling light and swiftly, countenancing no encumbrances until he could call himself safe from the law.

Abruptly Royal slammed both suitcases

shut and put them behind a couch. He turned to the others, his demeanour brooking no argument.

'It stays there for the moment,' he said flatly. 'In the morning we'll arrange for our getaway.'

'Morning!' Judge howled. 'Why wait until morning, Jack? Why not make the divvy right now and make it out of here while the going is good?'

'I go along with that,' Pete Kripp agreed.

'Are you all off your rockers?' Royal growled. 'If that guy in the car was a cop then the heat is on us. If we run out of here we run straight into the arms of the law. We're doing it my way. We're not going to panic. What use will the dough be if we smash ourselves up against the cops? As it is we're safe where we are. We've covered our tracks and we can afford to take the time to plan and plan well. What do you say, Brad ?'

Brad shrugged, seeing a lot of sense in the speech Royal had made.

'You could be right,' he acknowledged.

'Of course I'm right. So simmer down. Keep your cool.'

'What about the girl?' Brad asked him. 'When do we turn her loose and where?'

'I've got that worked out,' the squat man replied. 'Before we leave we'll fix the bolts so that they'll give when she throws herself at the door for a while. Once she's free she'll make her way to one of the other cabins.'

Brad was on the verge of objecting. It had been his idea to drive the girl into the suburbs of town and drop her there. But with the shift in circumstances this could prove foolhardy. Better to let Royal have his way.

It was late when Brad turned in for a sleep. He slept only fitfully and what sleep he did have was riddled with fearsome dreams.

He was glad when he opened his eyes to see the dawn. On his way to the bathroom he disturbed Kripp dozing on his stool.

'Wakey, wakey, Pete. Has the girl used the bathroom yet?'

Kripp shook his head sleepily.

'She never stirred the whole night.'

'I bet she could do with a mug of java.'

He helped Royal make breakfast in the kitchen, and when it was ready he carried a loaded tray into the corridor. Kripp rose and yawned.

'Hell, I'm bushed. I'm going to grab a couple of hours in the sack.'

Brad laid the tray down to release the bolts. He was surprised to discover that the inner lock wasn't on.

'Miss Regan...' he said, opening the door carefully. She lay across her bed. Brad smiled faintly, taking the tray on in and closing the door with his heel.

She sat up and stared blankly at him, and

he knew immediately that something was the matter. The girl's clothes were torn to ribbons and yet she made no effort to conceal her nakedness.

'Hello, Doris,' the girl said, still with that blank look in her eyes. 'Will you tell Daddy that I wish to talk with him.'

The tray slipped from Brad's fingers and clattered to the floor, spilling hot coffee over his feet. He went over to the girl and grasped her shoulders.

'What happened?' he cried hoarsely. 'Did some of those guys – Roy! It was Roy, wasn't it?'

'Doris, I want to see Daddy. Will you please tell Daddy to come here at once...'

Madness churning in his breast, Brad wheeled and rushed from the room, not bothering to close the door behind him. He stumbled back to the room he had slept in and withdrew his .38 from under the pillow. He met Pete Kripp in the doorway.

'Hey, what gives with you, Brad–'

Brad grabbed him and threw him aside. He crossed the passage to the room occupied by Roy Judge. Judge was fast asleep in bed and Brad slapped his face viciously to waken him.

Judge's head rolled before consciousness was forced on him and he opened his eyes wildly.

'You, Brad... What the hell is the matter?

212

What are you doing with that gun?' Judge's voice rose to a shriek.

'I'm going to kill you with it, you dirty bastard,' Brad said vibrantly. 'You raped her, didn't you, you filth?'

'No, no, I didn't! You've got it all wrong, Brad. Wait a minute and I'll explain…'

'Explain to Satan,' Brad said forcefully and shot Judge twice in the centre of his face.

CHAPTER FIFTEEN

Wesley Regan came to an abrupt halt and raised his head. Above the muted boil and roar of the ocean beating at the cliffs, and the thrum of automobile traffic, he fancied he had just heard a gunshot from somewhere behind him.

Tensed up to the limit as he already was, the new danger caused his heart to beat madly against his ribs, Cold sweat filmed his forehead and jaws. He was aware of the pull of his calf muscles. It showed him that his physical condition was not what he imagined. But then, what could take the stress which he had been subjected to during these last few days and not betray some evidence of all that strain?

No other similar sounds followed. It could have been a car backfiring, he realised. He didn't think so. He was sure that, following on the cracking noise, there had been some sort of crash.

What could have gone wrong? Surely Dick Knight hadn't been trailing him and had decided to have a showdown with the kidnappers when they revealed themselves?

No, Dick wouldn't do that. Anyhow, the

cop had no idea of what arrangements the kidnappers had made with him. Perhaps the kidnappers had been too eager to get their hands on the suitcases containing the money and had crashed. That would be an excuse for applause. Or would it? What about Carol? Until his daughter was returned to him, safe and sound, he didn't want anything to interfere with the kidnappers' plans.

Cuffing his cold, damp brow, Regan turned about and began walking slowly back to where he had left the Buick. If his return should prove premature and there was sign of the kidnappers in the vicinity, he would spot them before they spotted him and hang off until they took their leave.

Regan halted when he saw his car and stood still for a while, peering intently through the shadows. There was no movement of any description about the station wagon. So the kidnappers had come and gone. They must have come and gone. He had given them ample time to do what they had to do.

A car raced past him, too close for comfort. When the driver saw him he blew his horn fiercely. Regan wiped his brow again. He felt cold and hot at the same time. It was this kind of strain that could trigger off a heart attack. What had been the reason for the gunshot and the commotion which followed it?

The millionaire went on to the Buick, glancing all about him. He uttered a low curse when he saw the car crumpled up in the rocks above the ocean. With legs that grew weaker with every step, he approached the crashed car. It had crashed in there and it certainly hadn't been there on his arrival.

Now Regan fingered the gun in his pocket. Something had urged him to bring it along tonight just in case there was necessity to protect himself. He did not remove the gun from his pocket, but curled his finger on the trigger as he approached the car.

He stopped breathing when he looked into the car and saw the white, blood-streaked features of Dick Knight.

The nosy bastard! He really had caught on somehow that the ransom money was being delivered to the kidnappers. They had seen him, shot at him, causing him to crash and break his neck. Or maybe the gunshot had killed him.

Serve him right.

But the money – the suitcases... Had they been taken from the station wagon?

Regan staggered back to the Buick and looked for the suitcases. They had disappeared. The kidnappers had got the money anyhow, and that was something. But would they forgive him for calling on the aid of the cop, as they were bound to believe he had done?

At that moment a car slowed while the occupants stared out at him. It was a Highway Patrol car and Wesley Regan was sure he would expire. All the careful planning had come to nothing. In a few more minutes the kidnapping of his daughter would be blazed abroad.

But why should it be, he thought frantically. He might yet grasp the iron from the fire. If Dick Knight was dead and if Dick had kept what he had learned to himself, then there was no reason to tell anyone the whole truth.

The Highway Patrol vehicle nosed off the road and the two officers leaped out. They were tall and chunkily-built, and sight of them filled Regan with a vast dismay, despite his resolve.

'What's going on here?'

'I'm Wesley Regan,' Regan heard himself say in a hard voice. 'I was driving along when I saw that car over there. It must have crashed...'

'Is the driver in it?'

'Yes, he is. I think he is—'

'Go have a look-see, Mike.'

One of the officers hurried to the crashed car. The other looked from the Buick to the elderly man.

'You weren't involved in the crash, Mr. Regan?'

'No, of course I wasn't,' Regan snapped.

At that instant the officer at Dick's car shouted urgently. 'Hey, Fred, this guy is hanging on by a thread. Get an ambulance here fast.'

The officer went to his car and raised the controller. He spoke crisply for several minutes, then emerged. He saw Regan at the crashed car with Mike and made his way gingerly over the rocks. He thought there was something off-beam with the situation.

When Regan stared in at Dick he realised that his eyes were open. Mike warned him not to move.

'An ambulance will be here shortly, buddy. Just take it easy.'

'But – but–' Dick lifted himself on the seat despite the officer's warning. His brain was thick with fuzz and he had trouble bringing the dim faces into focus. When finally he recognised Wesley Regan his memory of events rushed back to him. The millionaire walking on the roadside. The parked Buick. That guy at the door of the station wagon. Then the windshield of his car shattering and the subsequent sickening crash.

'How did you get here, Dick?'

'You know who he is, Mr. Regan?' one of the officers said. 'But I thought... Look, buddy, stay there, will you? You might have broken bones. You took a bad jolt–'

Unheeding, Dick brushed the talk aside. When he insisted on sliding out of the driving seat they let him. Wesley Regan watched his efforts coldly, unsympathetic and condemning. Dick staggered and would have fallen had Mike not grabbed his arm.

Dick recovered and faced Regan. His nerves were on thin threads.

'Did – did they get the dough? You see, I–'

'You're finished with me, Knight. You may have balled up the whole works. I might never see my daughter again.'

'Your daughter?' Mike butted in. 'Say, will somebody tell me what is going on?'

'I'm Detective Sergeant Knight of the Kentburg force,' Dick explained hastily. 'I've got to get to your radio.'

'No!' Regan panted, gripping Dick's sleeve and wrestling with him. 'You've done enough damage. You're not going to set off any alarm. Hell, don't you understand what you're doing, Dick? My daughter ... Carol. They mightn't let her go now.'

'I'm sorry,' Dick said shakily. 'Not because I interfered. I had a duty to interfere. I love your daughter, sir. Those kidnappers won't release her, no matter what happens. They can't afford to release her.'

'Kidnappers!' Mike choked. 'Why didn't you say so? Let's put this in straightaway.'

He assisted Dick to the Highway Patrol car and then connected him with the controller. It was an effort for Dick to marshal his thoughts into a coherent pattern. They were eager to go on a trip.

'This is Detective Sergeant Knight of the Kentburg police department. Get a message through to Lieutenant Wills. Tell him I want every plug pulled on the Regan thing. The lieutenant will understand.'

'Very well, Sergeant.'

The scene swam around Dick. He was aware of Wesley Regan's fingers biting into his shoulder and of his rasping voice in his ear. But he was unable to make out what Regan was saying. Then there was another sound, that of a siren wailing its way to the spot. After that Dick lost consciousness.

Pete Kripp leaped on Brad from behind, managed to get a secure arm-lock on his neck, and hauled him away from the bed. In the brief struggle to release himself the gun fell from Brad's hand to the floor. A moment later Jack Royal was in the bedroom and had Brad covered with his own gun.

'Hold it, you stupid jerk,' Royal snarled at him. 'One more bad move and I'll gut-shoot you.' The squat man glanced at what had been Roy Judge's face and felt his blood turned to ice in his veins. 'Have you gone crazy or something?' he choked. 'Why did you want to kill him?'

The haze of madness receded from Brad's brain. He tugged deep gasps of air to his lungs. Roy Judge was a gory mess.

'He raped the girl,' he said hollowly. 'I told him to keep his hands off her, but he couldn't do it. The shock must have sent her out of her mind.'

'The hell he did!' Royal grated. Something in the other's eyes made him go on quickly. 'I didn't know, Brad. I haven't seen her. If he did it then he got nothing but what he deserves.'

Brad threw Kripp off him and confronted the two men. 'Listen,' he said forcefully, 'I've had a bellyful of this gag. It started off as a pretty sharp idea, maybe, but it has gone wrong. The deal was that the girl would go back to her old man the way we got her–'

'Yeah, yeah, I know, Brad. But nobody wanted this to happen. The dame has been raped and you've killed Roy. That makes for a swell variation, but I didn't ask for it. You say the shock has sent her round the bend? I don't believe it. I've never yet met the dame that would–'

'Go and look for yourself,' Brad interrupted him in turn. His voice rose to a high pitch. 'Go on and look!'

'All right, I will.'

Before Brad could guess his intention, Royal had scooped up his gun from the floor and stuffed it into his pocket. The two of them locked gazes for a throbbing moment.

'I don't want you getting too ambitious,'

the squat man said curtly. 'You'd better remember that.'

He wheeled and left the room and Brad's glare challenged Kripp. Kripp's sallow skin had gone a damp, yellowish shade. He forced a meagre grin and shrugged carelessly.

'One out and three to go,' he said with a mirthless chuckle. 'I sure hope we get value for murder, Brad. I know I've got a bad feeling along the place where my spine used to be.'

Brad thought he was going to be sick and had to get out of the bedroom. Kripp's eyes were muddy on his back.

He was in the living-room with Kripp when Royal returned from seeing how the girl was. He shook his head gloomily.

'Damned if I ever saw the likes of it.'

'She's actually flipped her lid?' Kripp asked incredulously. 'What the blazes did he do to her?'

'Forget it,' Royal responded with an angry wave of his hand. He unearthed the bottle which Judge had been drinking from and took a drink from the neck. He thought they really were in a hell of a mess. Now that Judge was dead, Pete would have to drive Brad through the hills to safety while he did away with the girl and set the cabin alight. He didn't relish the task, but it would have to be done. If the man in the car had been a cop then they could be sure that about now there was a full-scale search going on for them.

What should he do, he wondered, split the loot and send Pete and Brad packing at once? He would remain at the cabin until dusk, kill the girl and start a fire, then take off and get back to Swift's Beach as soon as possible.

He knew the cops would run a thorough check on everyone in the vicinity who had a questionable background. That included him. To keep in the clear he would have to make it to Darla's house in front of the cops. Darla would swear he had never been out of her sight. He could find a spot to bury the money and let it remain buried until the heat lifted. His tension slackened.

Pete and Brad were waiting expectantly for him to disclose his plans. Judging by the expression on Brad's face he was in the process of shaping plans of his own.

Royal went to the couch and lifted out one of the suitcases from behind it. He placed it on the floor.

'We can't afford to hang around any longer,' he said brusquely. 'There's half a million there. You guys take it with you and divide it. I take the rest.'

'You're welcome to it,' Brad returned flatly. 'But I'm not leaving here without the girl.'

Royal's eyes blazed at him. His mouth

narrowed to a tight trap.

'What? Are you completely nuts? I told you what I would do about the girl. I'll keep my promise. I'm staying here until dark. Roy being dead complicates things, alters things. I'm going to turn the girl free at dark. Then I'm going to put a match to the cabin. When they find what remains of Roy they'll surmise that the dame tricked him somehow and shot him. They'll fall for the whole gag and give us a chance to cover up our tracks.'

Kripp's gaze shuttled between Brad and the squat man. He knew what Jack really had in store for the girl, but he didn't give a curse so long as he got a head start on the cops.

'That's a bright thought, Jack,' he said with false enthusiasm. 'Okay, Brad, you can bank on Jack doing what he says he'll do. Let's grab this suitcase and skedaddle.'

Brad shook his head stubbornly.

'I'll leave when the girl leaves and not before. She's nothing better than an idiot, and I'm going to make sure she'll he taken back to her old man.'

'You stupid bastard,' Royal raged at him. He made an effort to control himself. So okay, if Brad wanted to act the hero, then he would have all the opportunity he needed. The big man was unarmed and he would simply keep him under close surveillance until dusk. After that he would go the way of Roy Judge, and there would be three charred skeletons dug out of the ruins instead of two. This would be all to the good, he decided. Then it would appear as if the men had fought and killed each other after killing the girl.

He mustered a feeble smile.

'All right, Brad, you can have your way. What are you going to do, Pete?'

'I know what I'm doing,' Kripp said with feeling. 'I'm making tracks from here as fast as I can. I'll find a sack or something to put my share in...'

He did find a sack and kneeled on the floor by the open suitcase to painstakingly divide the half million dollars.

Brad watched him with a sort of detachment, not really caring whether the money was equally divided. Brad had a premonition of disaster. They had got off to this on the wrong foot and it was too late now for them to get in step. But whatever happened, he intended ensuring that Carol Regan was restored to her father.

He stirred himself sufficiently to realise a danger in Kripp making off on his own.

'What happens if you're caught before you get out of the hills?'

Kripp's sallow cheeks turned fiery.

'What are you trying to wish on me, you punk? Don't you worry about me, pal, just think of yourself.'

'It's what I'm doing. If you're caught they'll make you talk.'

'They'll not make me talk, Brad. Anyway, any kind of risk is preferable to sharing the rest of the day with you ghouls.'

He drove away presently, watched from the front door by Royal and Brad. When he disappeared they went inside the cabin.

Brad extended his hand to Royal.

'Give me my gun, Jack.'

'What do you want with a gun?' the squat man demanded thinly. Just then he wouldn't trust Brad out of his sight.

'I might need it to defend myself. Give it to me.'

Royal handed the weapon over with bad grace. He advised Brad to keep his eyes peeled for the remainder of the day.

Towards evening Royal cooked a meal; he made no move to feed the girl until Brad placed some food on a tray and poured a cup of coffee. He carried the tray to the bedroom door, laying it on the floor while he threw back the bolts. The door opened as it had done earlier and Brad stepped through.

He came up short with a strangled cry when he saw the girl dangling from a hook on the wall, her toes just touching the floor.

She had used a length of curtain cord to hang herself.

CHAPTER SIXTEEN

Dick Knight was in the Central Hospital until early Monday morning. Had the doctor in charge been given his way Dick would have remained in hospital, under close observation, until it could be said with some degree of certainty that he had suffered nothing more serious than a mild concussion.

As it was, with six stitches in the head wound which had been caused, not by the bullet from Brad Gilbert's gun, but by being slammed forward to the steering wheel, he signed a form relieving the hospital of responsibility and had a cab drive him to police headquarters.

Here he sought out Lieutenant Wills. Wills was working in co-operation with Chief Pagano and an operation had been mounted that embraced all the resources of the department that could be made available. The F.B.I. had been alerted, and the overall mood relating to the kidnapping of the millionaire's daughter was one of hope.

Wills explained that Wesley Regan had decided to pitch in with his own knowledge and involvement.

'He sees there is nothing else for it, Dick.

But if the old gopher had come clean at the outset we might have apprehended the kidnappers by now.'

'What exactly has he told you?'

Wills gave Dick a detailed rundown. He had finished drawing up a list of likely suspects. Dick eyed the list and nodded grimly when he saw the names of Roy Judge and Bradford Gilbert.

'I'm certain that guy Gilbert is wrapped up in it, Lieutenant. This character Judge as well.'

'You could have given us the dope you picked up sooner. You ought to know by this time that a lone wolf goes hungry for most of the time. Look, Dick,' Wills added in a different tone, 'you're not quite up to the mark. Why don't you take a back seat and let us handle the case?'

Dick shook his head. He looked knocked-about and slightly bemused, but he knew he could never rest until Carol was retrieved from the clutches of the kidnappers.

'She's my girl, Lieutenant. Even if you order me off, I'll merely say the hell with the department and carry on from there.'

'All right. I'm not going to argue. I'm not going to throw my authority at you. Let's get weaving. The guy you saw on the road was alone, and there was no transport he could have used in sight?'

'I saw only the Buick station wagon. But

I've been thinking. The old Dorton road is elevated at the point where the lift was arranged. That's why they told Mr. Regan to stall where he did. Also, a short distance along, there is a fork that permits access to side roads that angle all over the country. As I see it, there could have been a car on the elevated road and perhaps another at the fork. The guy or guys in the car up above could have had a wide vision of the terrain. The one who went to lift the suitcases likely came from the high road when Mr. Regan had walked out of sight, as instructed.

'After throwing a slug at my car they had a car brought on in short order to take on the dough and the character who took it from the station wagon. Then they just buzzed off.'

Wills nodded slowly.

'It's the way it could have happened. If Regan had taken us into his confidence we could have thrown a cordon over the entire locality. We could have got those punks for sure.'

'Maybe, Lieutenant. But there was his daughter to consider. Listen ... I'm going to copy your list. I've got a strong hunch about Gilbert and Judge. That makes two of them. I'd say there were three at least, and perhaps four. If I can link Gilbert or Judge with other names–'

'I can't see how even that will assist us in

finding your girl, Dick,' Wills cut in. 'But go ahead, anyhow, by all means.'

Dick realised why he wanted him to go ahead with checking out the names on the list. If he was thus occupied it would keep him out of the feet of what Wills would call the experts.

He didn't mind. He had a few ideas of his own. If he could discover who else, besides Gilbert and Judge, was in on the kidnapping, there was the possibility of the knowledge giving him a pointer to the whereabouts of Carol.

He talked for several more minutes with the lieutenant, then lit a cigarette and rose to leave. At the door of the office he glanced back at Wills.

'Do you figure they'll return Carol as they promised they would?'

Wills shrugged and evaded his eyes.

'You never can tell, Dick. They may turn her loose.'

'Still, it's rarely in the character of kidnappers to release a victim that could finger them out.'

The lieutenant met his gaze squarely.

'You're a cop, Dick. You're trained to be realistic. I hate like hell not being able to offer you a grain of comfort, but you can chalk up the score for yourself.'

'Sure,' Dick said harshly, leaving the office and closing the door on his heels.

He spent the rest of the morning in combing the haunts frequented by men who, if they weren't actually denizens of the underworld, had a direct access to it. By noon he had marked off four of the names on his list. He had met these men and talked with them, and he was satisfied of their innocence of implication in the snatching of Carol Regan. There were a dozen more suspects to be investigated.

He grabbed a meagre lunch at a diner, then went straight to work again.

Lieutenant Wills had given him a plain car equipped with a radio link with headquarters, and he called through every hour to be apprised of developments. So far not a clue had been uncovered.

It looked pretty hopeless, Dick reflected bitterly. He had reached the stage where he dared not think of Carol's plight. An ungovernable anger assailed him when he did so, and then he had to wallow in a sense of frustration and impotence.

In the middle of the afternoon he caught a whisper that might provide a lead. According to his informant, Roy Judge and Jack Royal had been seen together a lot of late. Royal was one of the men named on the list Dick carried, and he thought it might be worth a try.

As things stood, he was prepared to grasp

at the slimmest hope.

Dick knew that once upon a time Jack Royal had lived in a cheap hotel in the skid-row area of Kentburg, but since the death of his sister's husband he had gone to live at her home on Swift's Beach. He got into his car and drove to Swift's Beach. He was not aware of the exact location of the sister's house, but he had it pointed out to him.

The frame building looked deserted as he climbed the steps to the front door. The sky out to seaward had dulled over and there was the threat of rain in the air. Dick pressed at the discoloured ivorine bell button and waited.

After a minute the door opened on a sensual-looking woman who regarded the detective suspiciously. Her breath smelled of liquor and she swayed slightly towards him.

'Excuse me,' she said with a weak smile. 'But I haven't been feeling well. What can I do for you?'

'My name is Knight. I take it you are Mrs. Grant, Mrs. Darla Grant?'

'You take it on the nose, buster.' For all her effort at carelessness Dick detected a definite uneasiness in her manner. But what was she worried about, he wondered. She continued to stand in a position where she was blocking the doorway, and it was evident that visitors weren't welcome at the moment.

'Then you are the sister of Jack Royal?'

'And you are a cop?' she countered, casting aside whatever role she had planned to adopt. 'What do you want with Jack? But before you answer that, I'd better tell you he isn't at home.'

'Oh? So he doesn't live here any more?'

'What do you want with him?'

Dick flashed his badge. She endeavoured to focus on it before shifting her attention to his face.

'I'd like to know where he is, Mrs. Grant. Could I – uh – come in and talk with you?'

She hesitated while she thought it over. At length she frowned and stepped aside.

'Okay, handsome, come in. Not that I can guess what good it's going to do for you. Still, I have nothing to hide, mister. Nothing at all.'

'My name is Dick.' He grinned as he said it. The woman's full lips bent in a smile.

'You're nice for a cop.'

'I won't keep you long.'

She led him into the living-room. It was a mess. *True Confession* mags were scattered around a couch. There was a coffee table next the couch but it held a bottle of gin that had been raided three-quarter-ways down, three empty tonic bottles and a misted glass. A house-coat had been balled and tossed into a corner.

The woman shrugged apologetically.

'You've caught me at a bad time, like I said. Usually I have the place shipshape at this time of day.'

'Forget it, Mrs. Grant.'

She sank down on a busted lounging chair and Dick took an upright chair opposite her. He extended his cigarette case. 'Smoke?'

'Thanks.' She took a cigarette and he held his lighter for her. She was a woman who was bored to tears with her life, he told himself. Maybe she had been something different when her husband was alive, but just now she was a gilt-edged slut.

She lay back on her chair and dragged at the cigarette. She blew the smoke across into Dick's face. After a moment she sat forward and regarded him steadily.

'Okay, Dick,' she said in a husky voice, 'let's hear the worst.'

'The worst?' He was aware of a needling of excitement which he made a big effort to conceal. 'You mean you were expecting to hear of your brother being in trouble?'

'If he isn't in trouble, why are you here?'

Dick tried to appear calm and at ease. There were two tacks he could try on her. He could bulldoze the woman in the hope of her explaining what Royal had been up to, or he could probe gently, not going too deep and not getting her hackles up. He decided on the latter course.

'At the minute I can't say whether Jack is

in trouble, Mrs. Grant. I hope he isn't–'

'What a hope!' she said sourly and blew more smoke into his face. 'Look, Dick, you don't have to pull your punches with me. I've lived with Jack for long enough to expect anything of him at any moment. Just give it to me on the chin, but I must tell you, buster, that I'm no chiseller. He is my brother after all.'

'Of course.' Dick arranged his thoughts rapidly. The woman was studying the scar on his forehead now. She ran her tongue across her lips. 'Well, Mrs. Grant, I'd like to put a few simple questions to you concerning your brother. There is nothing to be afraid of if you tell me the truth.'

'You must be kidding,' she said derisively. 'And what happens if I don't want to tell you the truth?'

'Then I'll have to ask you to come down to headquarters with me,' Dick returned bluntly. 'So what is it to be, ma'am?'

'Oh, okay. I guess what's happened has happened and nothing I say will alter it.'

'You're being wise, Mrs. Grant. Now, tell me, when did you last see your brother?'

'Let me think... What day is this –Monday, as if I didn't know! I hate Mondays, Dick. Don't ask me why. Well, it must have been Friday when he left– No, that isn't so. It was Thursday.'

Dick's heart began thumping against his

ribs. The woman sloshed gin into her glass and took a long pull. She laid the glass down, wiped her lips with the back of her hand.

'You're sure it was Thursday?'

'Yes, I am sure. I haven't seen Jack since. But this isn't strange, you understand. He goes off occasionally. He might be gone for a day, two days, a week. It's a free country after all, and I'm only his sister.'

'Was he alone when he left? I mean, did he mention that he was seeing someone?'

It filtered through to Darla that the cop didn't know as much about Jack as he pretended to know. She could smell a tall bluff as well as the next person, and nice guy or no nice guy, he was a cop, and he was trying to nail Jack's hide to a fence.

'How the hell do I know?' she said sullenly.

Dick stood up and the woman started. The smile had left his features and he was now grim and threatening.

'You'd better get your coat, Mrs. Grant.'

'Hey, are you kidding?'

'I'm not kidding. If you refuse to talk here, then you'll talk at headquarters. Come on–'

'No, wait!' she panted, rising and catching his sleeve. 'If you'll just tell me why you're interested in Jack...'

Dick made a rapid decision.

'I'll tell you why. Wesley Regan's daughter

was kidnapped on Thursday night. The kidnappers demanded and collected the sum of a million dollars. So you see, this isn't a case of being involved in stealing peanuts, Mrs. Grant. This is a federal offence. If your brother is innocent, then there's nothing to worry about. But if he's guilty he deserves to be caught and he's going to be caught, come hell or high water.'

'Kidnap!' Darla echoed and slumped down on her chair. She shook her head violently, going on in a flat monotone as though talking to herself, 'I knew there was something bad in the wind. I just knew it. I talked with him ... I told him he would catch it in the neck one of these days.'

'Was he alone when he left, Mrs. Grant?'

'What?' Darla shuddered and stared at the detective. She moved her head to and fro, gently now. 'No, he wasn't alone. I had the feeling they were cooking up something.'

'Who was? Your brother and who else?'

'Pete Kripp for one,' the woman answered blankly. 'And Roy Judge. But they're pals of Jack. Then he brought this other guy to the house ... a total stranger. Well, almost...'

'What was his name?' Dick was like a greyhound on the leash just then. He prayed that the woman would remember the name of the fourth man.

'His name was Gilbert. Brad Gilbert–'

'Listen,' Dick said brusquely, 'I'm going to

search this house, Mrs. Grant. You can object if you want to, but I'll soon have a warrant to give me the authority.'

'Why do you wish to search? What do you hope to find – evidence to send Jack to the gas chamber?'

'Evidence to prove one thing or another,' Dick retorted. 'If he's in the clear he has nothing to be afraid of.'

'But what if he isn't in the clear? What if he is mixed up in the kidnapping?'

Dick had no answer for that one. He saw that the woman was close to tears. But what was her position when compared with the jam that Carol Regan was in? There was really no comparison.

'Can I search or can't I?'

'Okay, okay, go ahead and search. Make it tough for yourself. There's no telling what Jack will do when he hears how you muscled in here.'

It was enough for Dick.

'Show me to his bedroom first of all. Then to any other room he might have used exclusively.'

'He did have a sort of office... Oh, lord what am I saying! I don't want Jack to be in trouble.'

'Keep your fingers crossed that he isn't.'

She showed him her brother's bedroom and the detective went through it thoroughly. He couldn't say what he was looking for. Just anything to tie Royal in solidly with the kidnapping. He didn't find it. His spirits faltered.

'This office,' he grunted at length. 'You haven't cleaned it since he went away?'

It was a superfluous query, but she confirmed his guess with a shake of her head. She stood by the door while he searched. She asked him for a cigarette and he obliged.

Stuff had been burned in the fireplace, Dick noted, but there wasn't enough ash to determine what it had been other than paper.

He found a scrap of paper lodged at the back of a drawer. It was folded in four and he opened it out. A printed receipt from a concern called Pine Lake Enterprises. He was in the process of refolding it when he noticed the name typed on the receipt. Jack Wade, Kingston.

He looked at Dana.

'Who's Jack Wade?'

'I never heard of a Jack Wade.'

'You never saw this receipt before?' He extended it to her and she took it in trembling fingers. There was something relentless about this man that frightened her.

'I never saw it. I know nothing about it.'

Dick recovered the receipt. His brow corrugated in a frown of concentration. Pine Lake Enterprises? It rang a bell somehow. Of course! It was a vacation centre up in the hills. A lot of cabins scattered over a wooded area. What better place for a band of kidnappers to use as their hideout!

An eager light glinted in Dick's eye now.

'I want to use your phone, Mrs. Grant,' he said urgently.

'Why not? You're practically my guest. But what has that got to do with Jack?'

'I'm going to find out.'

Hunched over the phone table he dialled the operator and explained that he wished to make a long distance call.

'To Pine Lake Enterprises, Los Angeles. Here is the number...'

For the next five minutes he was engaged on the phone. Finally he slapped down the instrument and spun to the door. Darla Grant called after him.

'Are you all through here?'

'For the present,' he shouted back. 'Don't make any attempt to leave town, Mrs. Grant...'

CHAPTER SEVENTEEN

'We've really had it now,' Brad said to Royal in a hollow voice. 'With the girl dead, the cops and the F.B.I. will turn this country inside out to find us.'

'The cops don't know the girl is dead,' Royal argued. It didn't matter to him one way or the other that she had hanged herself. It would save him the trouble of killing her. Now he had only Brad to take care of. 'The cops are completely in the dark regarding our whereabouts,' the squat man went on. 'They don't have a clue to who is responsible for the snatch.' He wondered if he shouldn't spare Brad. He liked the big man in a way. He had guts and a lot of intelligence, and perhaps he was entitled to his place in the sunshine. But then he thought of Brad's sole weakness: it was this conscience thing that he had. Just because they had promised to return the dame to her father in return for the money, he was down in the mouth about their failure to do so.

Royal decided he mustn't forget, either, how Brad had flashed his wad around after the hijacking of his truck. If he did that with his share of the loot, he wouldn't only be a hazard to himself but to him and Pete as well.

No, Royal told himself, Brad Gilbert must die. And it would have to be done shortly. The sooner he got back to Swift's Beach and Darla's house the more secure would be his position.

Outside, the sky was gradually darkening.

The two stiffs in the house gave Royal a fit of the creeps. Roy lay in bed where he had died, his face a bloody unrecognisable mask. At this minute the room buzzed with flies. Brad had cut the girl down at once and made a desperate attempt to resuscitate her. He had laid off only when his body was running with sweat and the hard truth came through to him. The beautiful blonde girl would never breathe again.

Her death did something terrible to Brad. He appeared to have lost his final spark of enthusiasm for the whole business. Even his dreams of getting out of the country and settling somewhere in riches and comfort had become little better than a heap of ashes. He would never be able to rid himself of Carol Regan's ghost, of the vision of her hanging there on the wall, her face swollen and contorted; her bulging, accusing eyes would follow him to his grave.

Royal made coffee in the kitchen and invited Brad to share it. The big man was in the initial stage of disintegration, Royal noted. Some of these big, tough guys were nothing but mush inside. Brad could flip his lid and go berserk at a moment's notice, and then he certainly would have his hands full.

'Just forget it, Brad, huh? Drink this up and pull yourself together. You didn't kill her; I didn't kill her. It was Roy who did the trick and now he's dead too.'

Brad considered the squat man. He had known Jack Royal to be hard and ruthless, but he hadn't suspected his total lack of warmth and feeling. Jack would take his half million bucks and have a ball spending it. When he left this cabin he would shut a door behind him that he would never think of opening again.

Brad drank the coffee. It helped thaw the block of ice he was carrying around for a stomach. An unusual noise caused him to jerk upright and stare at Royal.

'What the hell is that?'

Royal had heard also and raised his head in an attitude of listening. A paleness crawled into his cheeks and fear touched his eyes.

'A motor,' he said hoarsely. 'It seems to be practically overhead...'

'It's a chopper!' Brad yelled and started for the door.

Royal followed him to the porch and they peered up at the darkening heavens. The lights of the hovering helicopter were visible.

Royal gave a harsh laugh

'Calm down. It's an army chopper, likely. They take spells of buzzing around.'

'Maybe,' Brad gritted thickly. 'Maybe not. Maybe that cop friend of the girl's has got on to us. Maybe Pete drove into a road block and has spilled his guts.'

'Don't be so goddamned stupid,' Royal raved. Yet he was as worried as Brad. They watched the helicopter circle the woods, drop low over the trees, and then glide off out of sight.

Brad's jaws were streaming with sweat. He turned back into the house. Royal went after him.

'What are you going to do?'

'The radio,' Brad hustled. He glanced at his watch.

'Almost on the hour. We might catch something on the news.'

Royal had an urge to shoot him right now and be done with him. If he didn't do it soon he might miss his chance, and then his entire escape effort could be complicated to the point of disaster.

He stood above Brad at the table as he twiddled with the knobs of the portable radio.

A hideous commercial filled the room. The burbling voice of the guy doing the spiel was sickeningly incongruous. A storm of canned music followed, faded, and the newscaster came on.

'This is station XB LKN, with the news on the hour. The police report definite progress on the Carol Regan kidnapping. When the news of the kidnapping broke every force in the county went into action. Road blocks have been erected over a wide area and the police say they have hopes of early arrests being made– Flash! A note has just come to my desk. A man has been apprehended with a car containing what is believed to be his share of the ransom money. Information is requested on three other men. Jack Royal, who is aged forty—'

Royal reached over and snapped off the switch. A raw oath rolled from his lips.

'They're on to us, Brad! They've caught Pete and they're on to us. The goddamn bastard has told them everything. The helicopter was making a reconnaissance of the cabin. They'll have spotted my car and reported the fact.'

It was true, Brad thought numbly; it just had to be true. He listened for sounds of the helicopter, but heard nothing.

His face was grey as he rose from the table. His mouth had hardened to a bitter line.

'It looks like your plan has failed, Jack.'

'Is that all you can say?' Royal snarled at him. 'You think I'm beaten, don't you?

You're going to sit here and wait till they come and get you...'

'Are you nuts?' Brad demanded coldly. 'I've been in jams before, mister. Plenty. I've never tossed in my hand before, and I'm not doing it now. We're going to load the money into your car and we're going to make a damn good try at getting clear.'

'Let's hustle then,' Royal jerked out. 'We don't have a minute to spare.'

He watched Brad go to the couch and lean over it to haul up the suitcases. For a brief second indecision clutched Royal and held him. Then he drew his gun from his pocket and snicked off the safety.

'Can't that guy drive any faster?' Dick Knight was saying to the man beside him in the rear seat of the car.

'He's going fast enough, Dick,' Lieutenant Wills returned thinly. 'This is no road for taking liberties on.'

'Those jerks on the radio,' Dick panted angrily. 'I thought you were keeping the manoeuvre sewed up until we were ready to make the strike?'

'Don't blame me,' Wills grumbled. 'Blame the Chief. Once he took the reins in his hands he became the boss. Anyhow, he's getting results. Kripp was trapped at that roadblock, wasn't he? These hills are sealed off so that a rabbit couldn't get out of them without being scrutinised. But I wouldn't bet on the rest of the gang being at the cabin.'

'Carol will be there,' Dick groaned. 'Heaven knows what will have happened to her by this time.'

'Just relax, will you? While there's life there's hope.'

Even as he spoke Wills reflected that there was small chance of the Regan girl being discovered alive. Once the kidnappers became desperate they would make every possible effort to cover up their tracks.

The cop at the wheel pointed to a speck of light in the sky.

'There's the army chopper,' he sang back at them.

'It's getting too dark for it to be of much use,' Dick lamented. 'All it'll do is make those guys panic – if they haven't been tuned in to the radio. If they have, they're already warned.'

'It was the Federal agent's idea,' Wills murmured. He was straining his eyes to watch the helicopter. The pilot had orders to keep them informed.

The radio crackled and Dick leaned forward.

'This is Sergeant Brody reporting ... this is Sergeant Brody...'

'Come in, Sergeant,' Dick snapped into the mike.

'Have you got any readings?'

'Have just made a recce over the marked area,' Brody's voice droned. 'There is a car parked at the cabin. Shall I go back to hovering at the scene?'

Wills grabbed the mike from Dick's fingers.

'Lieutenant Wills speaking. No. Keep back from the scene. If I need you I'll buzz. Hold yourself in readiness.'

'Understood, Lieutenant. Over and out.'

'That means some of the hoods are still at the cabin,' Dick cried excitedly. 'Jim, it's possible that Carol is okay.'

'Yeah,' Wills grunted shortly. He was thinking they had no way of knowing how many of the kidnappers remained at the cabin. They might have a car apiece, and the one spotted by the 'copter could have refused to start. He was frankly apprehensive of what they might find at the cabin, but he didn't say so.

The dipped lights of the three carloads of armed officers following them dashed off the rear window on a straight. Dick looked at his watch and then studied the road ahead. They were travelling through a tunnel of trees.

'It can't be far to Pine Lake now,' he said musingly.

'I make it a short mile from where we are,' the driver said over his shoulder. 'What's the procedure?'

'I'll tell you in a moment, John. Keep hitting the gas.'

When the lieutenant saw the first of the cabins he barked a sharp order.

'Okay, John. Kill the engine and lights. Dick, climb out and flag them down. Organise the boys in a group and hold them for me.'

Dick sprang to the road without answering. Wills narrowed his eyes on the map of the Enterprises' site he had clipped to a board. He noted the road they were on and marked the cabin in front of them in relation to it. His ballpoint danced across the tiny squares that represented the cabins. The one which had been rented to Jack Wade bore a thick cross, and would be away down near the lake. He hoped the whole exercise didn't turn out to be a waste of time and the kidnappers weren't forty miles away on the other side of the hills. Dick wanted blood and Dick ought to get blood.

Wills hoped, too, that it wasn't the dame's blood Dick saw first.

He got out of the car.

A score of armed officers stood tensely at the ready. None of them had so much as a word to say. Wills couldn't help but feel impressed.

'Boone, you peel off four men and descend through the trees in a straight line until you sight the cabin. Charley, you take four and proceed a hundred yards along the road before you go down. Get the cabin in view and remain on the alert. Dick, you also take four and see if you can make your way to a point below the cabin. I and the rest of the boys will close in from the top. You all know the one we're referring to?'

'We've got a pretty good idea, Lieutenant,' Detective 2nd grade Boone responded.

'What about you, Charley?'

'I've studied the map, Lieutenant. It ought to be the last one before the lake on this side.'

'There's no doubt that it is,' Wills said curtly. 'Now, listen, I'm going to hail the cabin and give them a chance to come out. Don't open fire unless you're compelled to. Remember that the girl is probably in the cabin. If they play it dirty, she could be the first one to emerge. These considerations apart, prepare to defend yourselves. Get going, and don't forget your Fenimore Cooper Indians. They didn't blow bugles.'

Wills noticed Dick's indecision, but turned his back on him. When he glanced across his shoulder Dick was leading his men away. The men who were left waited for his orders.

'Just a second, fellas.'

Wills went to the car and raised the helicopter. He issued terse instructions.

'Give us exactly ten minutes and then

zoom in on that cabin. Scare the hell out of them so they'll break for the open.'

'Ten minutes it is, Lieutenant.'

Wills emerged.

'Come on, fellas. Let's weave.'

Faint as the clicking of the safety was, Brad heard it and alarm streaked along his nerves. He was holding the heavier of the suitcases, and flung it at Royal with all his strength. The gun banged and the bullet slammed into the tough leather.

Before Royal could gather his wits Brad leaped on top of him and they went to the floor in a confusion of arms and legs.

After a hectic struggle Brad managed to secure a purchase on Royal's right wrist. The muzzle was being forced with a super-human strength towards his face. Royal's face was writhing with the frustration and fury that possessed him. Sweat rolled off his jaws and the thick veins in his neck corded into ropes.

'You – tricky – bastard, Jack...'

Brad smashed his left fist at the man's face and felt it connecting with bone and flesh. The gun erupted and a bullet screamed past his forehead. The powder burn was enough to send him lunging backwards. He re-covered as Royal strove mightily to draw a proper bead. The gun blasted once more, the slug missing him, but the powder flash practically blinding him.

With an agonised scream he sprang bodily on top of the squat man. The hard metal of the gun dug into his groin. There was a smothered roar, a harsh, strangled gasp, and the body beneath him went slack and lifeless.

Brad dragged himself upright, blinking frantically in an endeavour to see what had happened. Royal had shot himself in the stomach and was as dead as a dodo.

Brad dragged air into his lungs. He heard the chatter of the helicopter's engine again. The noise filled him with dread. The chopper seemed to be directly above the cabin. He had to get out of here, and fast.

He was charging for the door when he remembered the suitcases. Imagine going through what he had suffered and then forgetting the money!

When he reached the door with the suitcases he froze. Hell. He must not go out there at all. Those guys in the chopper would gun him down on the minute he showed.

An amplified voice sent his heart plunging.

'Hello, in there! Listen ... this is the police. We want to do a deal with you. Send the girl out first, and then come after her with your hands in the air... Hello! If you are agreeable, make a signal that you are. Flash a light. Open the door wide and show yourself...'

'The bastards!' Brad panted brokenly. 'The unmitigated bastards. They've got me pinned down. Pete must have spilled everything to them. I hope he rots. But I'm not going to rot... If I can only make it to the car I'll drive clean through them.'

He hung there against the door, a queer torpor invading his senses. It was as though he had known all along that the trick was doomed to failure, and his system had been geared to cope with the inevitable.

No. That sort of thinking was death. You had to stand up and fight back. If you didn't assert what you were, and what you stood for as a person, the world would run over you and bulldoze you into the mud.

He had had a bellyful of mud.

He gripped the lighter of the suitcases. Overhead, the grating clamour of the helicopter contrived a weird background to the speculations which plagued him, to the emotions which insisted on dominating his powers of reasoning.

With a shrill battle-cry pealing from his lips he hauled the door open, clattered down the steps, and rushed towards Jack Royal's car.

A voice called on him to halt and raise his arms. He screeched a defiant curse at the anonymous shadows. Now he was at the car and clawing at the door on the driving side. The door wouldn't budge, and with a stab of utter dismay he realised that Royal must have locked it.

Forms materialised out of the darkness. They seemed to be closing in on him from every conceivable angle.

'Just stand where you are, mister. That's it. That's it. Put your arms above your head.'

Brad did so. There might be some way out for him, he thought. He didn't want to die yet, did he? No, he didn't want to die yet.

He was slumped over the hood of the car when Dick Knight reached him. He was sobbing like a child who had lost everything.

Other officers tightened in on the cabin.

The publishers hope that this book has given you enjoyable reading. Large Print Books are especially designed to be as easy to see and hold as possible. If you wish a complete list of our books please ask at your local library or write directly to:

Dales Large Print Books
Magna House, Long Preston,
Skipton, North Yorkshire.
BD23 4ND

This Large Print Book, for people
who cannot read normal print,
is pub...   ...f

THE ULV...   ...ION

... we hope...   ...ook.
Please think...   ...ose
who have w...   ... ...
and are un...   ...njoy
Large Print...   ...ty.

You can h...   ...a
donatio...

**The Ulver...   ...n,
1, The Gre...   ...d,
Anstey, Leicestershire, LE7 7FU,
England.**
or request a copy of our brochure for
more details.

The Foundation will use all donations
to assist those people who are visually
impaired and need special attention
with medical research, diagnosis
and treatment.

Thank you very much for your help.